THE SECRET LANE

D1251590

Cover: View of Nettleton, Wiltshire,
from a painting by the late Cyril Rice.
(By courtesy of Mrs Eileen Rice).

Ralph Whitlock

The Secret Lane

A Country Story

Ralph Whitlock

Ex Libris Press

First published in 1990 by
Ex Libris Press
1 The Shambles
Bradford on Avon
Wiltshire

Typeset in 11 point Plantin by
Manuscript, Trowbridge
Cover printed by Devenish & Company, Bath
Printed in Great Britain by BPCC Wheatons Ltd, Exeter

ISBN 0 948578 22 X

CONTENTS

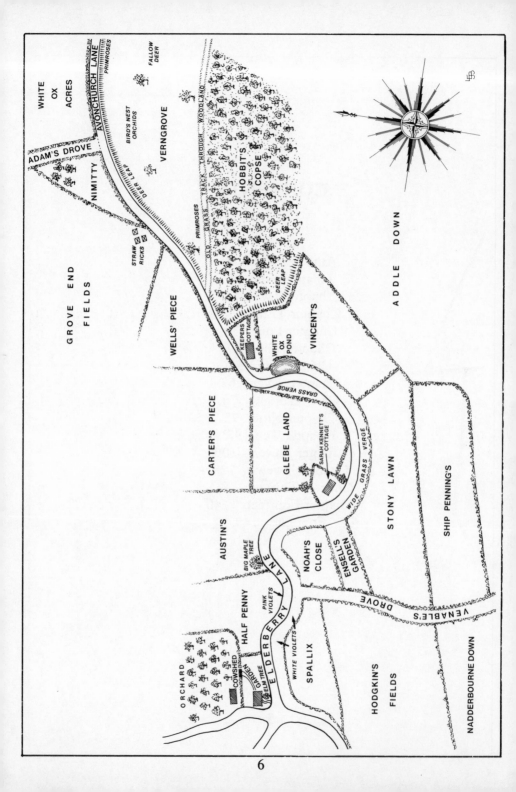

WHITE OX ACRES

AVONCHURCH LANE

PRIMROSES

PRIMROSES

FALLOW DEER

BIRD'S NEST ORCHIDS

VERNGROVE

ADAM'S DROVE

NIMITY

DEER LEAP

STRAW RICKS

GROVE END FIELDS

OLD GRASS TRACK THROUGH WOODLAND

HOBBIT'S COPSE

PRIMROSES

DEER LEAP

WELLS' PIECE

KEEPERS COTTAGE

WHITE OX POND

VINCENT'S

ADDLE DOWN

GRASS VERGE

CARTER'S PIECE

GLEBE LAND

SARAH KENNETT'S COTTAGE

WIDE GRASS VERGE

STONY LAWN

SHIP PENNING'S

AUSTIN'S

BIG MAPLE TREE

NOAH'S CLOSE

ENSELL'S GARDEN

PINK VIOLETS

HALF PENNY

ELDERBERRY LANE

WHITE VIOLETS

SPALLIX

VENABLE'S DROVE

ORCHARD

COWSHED

GARDEN

ELM TREE

HODGKIN'S FIELDS

NADDERBOURNE DOWN

6

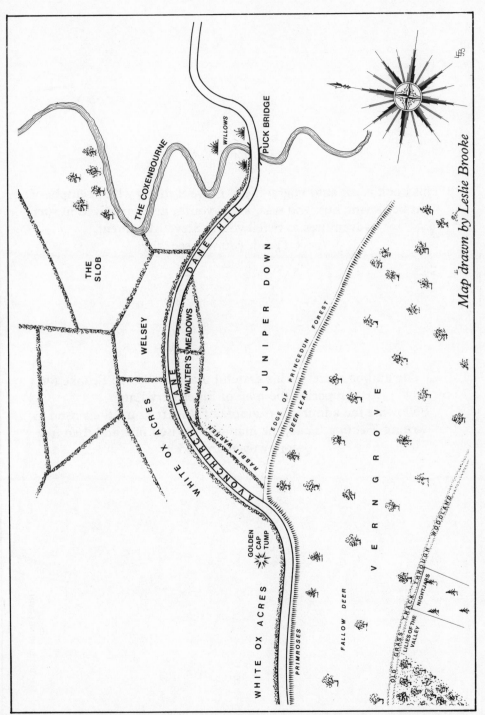

Map drawn by Leslie Brooke

THE COXENBOURNE

WILLOWS

PUCK BRIDGE

THE SLOB

DANE HILL

WELSEY

WALTER'S MEADOWS

JUNIPER DOWN

EDGE OF PRINCEDUN FOREST

DEER LEAP

WHITE OX ACRES

AVONCHURCH LANE

RABBIT WARREN

VERNGROVE

GOLDEN CAP TUMP

WHITE OX ACRES

PRIMROSES

FALLOW DEER

OLD GRASS TRACK THROUGH WOODLAND

LILIES OF THE VALLEY

NIGHTJARS

7

Author's Note

This book is *not* autobiographical. I owe it to my wife to emphasise that her loving husband was, in his youth, never involved in such adventures as befell young Steve Maidment.
As you read, you will see why.

The author expresses his grateful thanks to Leslie Brooke for preparing the map of Elderberry Lane.
Following the admirable example of Robert Louis Stevenson in writing *Treasure Island*, the map was devised first and then the story woven around it!

Chapter One

"March comes in like a lion and goes out like a lamb," is a regularly quoted saying in Nadderbourne. Every year , at some time between March 1st and 31st, the winds stop blustering and shouting, the frosts dissolve in dew, and summer comes striding in with a smiling, illusory confidence. For a few days, perhaps five, perhaps as many as ten, the song-thrushes, the primroses, the queen bumble-bees, the pussy-willow catkins, the February-born lambs, the daisy-studded pastures, the iridescent mallard drakes and all awakening nature are sure that summer has come. While the hallucination lasts, the farmers use every hour of daylight to catch up on arrears of barley-sowing.

On this glowing March evening of 1930, however, having finished sowing in Pug's Close by five o'clock, my father had decided that it was too late to start cultivating another field that day. George and Jimmy were transferring the necessary implements to Eleven-acres and my father said,

"You'd better slip down to Uncle Walter's and see if he's got those pea-sticks ready."

"The peas are only just sown," I reminded him.

"I know. We ought to have chased him before now," said my father, "If we want those sticks before the peas are a foot high. You've got to keep prodding that latterlamsical old shirker."

"Did I hear you're going down to Uncle Walter's?" enquired my mother, appearing at the kitchen door. "Then ask Aunt Maria if she has any broody hens yet. We don't want that keeper to get them."

Broody hens were at a premium in March and April. Farmers' wives wanted them for incubating hens' eggs; the keeper, Henry

Upshot, for sitting on pheasant eggs. Later, of course, in May and June most of the hens would be broody, but by then the hatching season would be nearly over. So for the meagre supply of early broodies fairly intense rivalry existed, especially as Henry was not the most popular character in the village. Upholding zealously the interests of his employer, the Earl of Crewkerne, on the Princedun estate which impinged on the outskirts of our village, he went so far as to interfere with women and children picking primroses and lilies-of-the-valley in woods where they had been accustomed to do so from time immemorial. Such actions bred more acrimony by far than his occasional successful interception of village poachers, for whom the risk of being caught by the enemy added zest to the ancient sport.

Finding, rather surprisingly, that no-one had borrowed my bike, I vaulted into the saddle and free-wheeled down the hill to Uncle Walter's.

Uncle Walter lived in a thatched, mud-walled cottage on a bank at the junction between our road, which is the main one through Nadderbourne, and Elderberry Lane. You approached it by way of a wicket-gate under an immense elm-tree, which caused Aunt Maria sleepless hours on every stormy night. She feared, and not without reason, that one night a south-westerly gale would send the tree crashing across the cottage. It was futile, however, to talk to Uncle Walter about having the tree felled. He had inherited the cottage from Aunt Maria's father, and the elm was a feature which had probably existed as long as the building. Uncle Walter was a conservative. He liked things to remain as they always had been; besides which, the tree was useful to him. Leaning against it was a den — a roughly-thatched, board shed where he kept his wheelbarrow and gardening tools, also a collection of old flower-pots and seed-boxes, and a chair in which he could sit with his pipe, watching such traffic as used the road in those distant, quiet days.

You walked past this nest up the brick-surfaced path, with rows of vegetables in mathematical precision on either side, to the faded green front door. The outdoor privy and the pigsty were round the back, where space was found for a few more ranks of vegetables between the house and the low hedge, half-buried in periwinkles, which marked the boundary between the garden and the orchard and paddock beyond. Aunt Maria was allowed a narrow flower border, the boundaries of which were marked by large flints, under the windows and around the front door, and Uncle Walter begrudged her even that. He was a vegetable man.

The orchard and paddock, comprising about three acres, formed the nucleus of Uncle Walter's little "farm". It conformed almost exactly to the old Liberal ideal of five acres and a cow. Of Uncle Walter's five acres, three were here and two a mile-and-a-quarter down Elderberry Lane. This apparently awkward arrangement suited Uncle Walter very well, for the following reason.

For most of its length, Elderberry Lane possessed a wide grass margin, probably dating from past centuries when it ran across open prairie, before the land on either side was enclosed by hedges and carved into fields. Every morning, after milking his three cows, or such of them as happened to be in milk at the time, feeding the calves and pigs, eating breakfast and paying a visit to the privy, Uncle Walter set off to take his herd to the distant meadows. It was a leisurely pilgrimage. One was more likely to find Uncle Walter leaning against a gate, smoking his pipe and watching the cows graze on the spacious roadside than actually moving. The cattle derived far more of their sustenance from the grassy verges than from the tiny meadows which were their ultimate destination. The cows, who knew the routine, could be trusted to take their time. Sometimes, if a large calf were accompanying them, Uncle Walter kept it under control by a long rope, one end of which, tied around his waist, served the additional purpose of keeping his disintegrating old jacket in one piece.

By the time the cavalcade had reached the meadows and Uncle Walter had enjoyed a leisurely walk home, Aunt Maria had his lunch (or "dinner", to us country-folk) ready. He liked to sit for the best part of an hour, digesting the meal, before setting out for the meadows again. Taking their time, as on the outward journey, the cows grazed all the way home, arriving there at milking-time. For the night, they were turned into the home paddock.

There were, of course, some variations in this attractive recipe for an indolent, meditative life. At times when grass was scarce it was surprising how often the cows happened to find a gate open, allowing them into one of the meadows bordering Elderberry Lane. If the farmer who owned the meadow happened to spot them, Uncle Walter was, naturally, there, shouting at them and full of apologies for allowing them to stray.

"But there, I couldn't do nothing about it. Somebody's left the gate open."

Like most other villagers, Uncle Walter had wire snares and traps to attend to in the hedgerows. His two little meadows had wide hazel hedges, in which he cut supple rods for hurdle-making, bushy saplings for pea-sticks and bean-rods and brushwood for faggots for burning. This was winter and early spring work, and so, always one to attend to his own comfort, Uncle Walter had erected a little shelter of faggots, roofed with a few sheets of galvanised iron. Here he had a wooden chest for his tools and the inevitable hard-bottomed chair.

Back at home, in a lean-to attached to his ramshackle cowshed, he kept a portable cider-press, which he used for not only the apples from his own orchard but, on contract, for those of other villagers. The cider barrels occupied much of Aunt Maria's kitchen, forcing her to do her washing under the overhanging thatched eaves outside the back door. At busy seasons Uncle Walter could sometimes be persuaded to help neighbouring farmers in the harvest-fields or to do an acre or two of hoeing. In July he cut, with a scythe, the tall roadside grasses which were surplus to his cows' requirements and made a small rick of hay.

All in all, though, Uncle Walter never overworked himself. His was an easy-going philosophy, which served him very well, and Aunt Maria had learned to live with it.

But it would be wrong to think that Uncle Walter lacked ambition. He was motivated by the commonest of all human desires, to get rich quick, and without having to work hard for his fortune. Long ago, a tantalising prize had been dangled before his eyes. The lane had a secret , a treasure. If only he could find it he would be immensely wealthy.

So, strolling backwards and forwards along the lane, four times a day, in spring, summer, autumn and winter, for year after year, Uncle Walter searched for the treasure. He poked and probed into every corner which seemed to offer possibilities, and when he leant against a gate, pulling at his filthy old pipe, he was not necessarily philosophising about the meaning of life or even drinking in the beauty of the countryside around Nadderbourne but was more likely to be thinking of where else he might search and of what form the treasure might take. He had lived with it so long that it had become an obsession.

I knocked at the dusty green door, opened it, and called out to Aunt Maria.

"Come along in, Steve," she chanted in reply, having recognised my voice.

She was in the living-room, liberally sprinkled with flour and rolling out pastry, with a wooden rolling-pin, on a table which had had much of its surface worn away by years of scrubbing. The cider casks had long since elbowed her out of the kitchen for all but the most basic culinary operations.

"Where's Uncle Walter?" I enquired and thought immediately how unnecessary it was to ask.

"Out in the cowshed, milking. He's only just back."

"A bit late for him, isn't it? Has he been cutting our pea-sticks?"

"Not that I've heard of. Why, are you wanting some?"

"Dad gave him the order back in January. A dozen bundles. I'll bet he hasn't started them yet."

"You may be right, at that. Your uncle likes time to think about these things."

"You're sure he's not thinking more about that treasure? No signs of it yet, I suppose?"

"What do you think? But you musn't laugh at him , Steve. It keeps him happy."

"That'll be a lark if he does come across it one day. What do you think, Auntie? Is there anything there for him to find?"

Aunt Maria shook her head; then raised a floury elbow to brush aside a stray wisp of hair.

"I don't know, Steve. I really don't know. Sometimes I think he's found it already."

I stared at her in disbelief, and she went on,

"I mean, see how contented it has kept him all these years. It's kept his mind occupied ever since we came to live in this house, nearly forty years ago. Forty years of contented married life can be reckoned a bit of a treasure, as I hope you'll find out for yourself one day."

That sort of philosophising went over the head of an eighteen-year-old. My thoughts were still engaged with chests of buried gold.

"What was it Aunt Sarah really said about it?

"Not much. It was just that one day, when we were talking about getting hold of a bit more land — that big field at the edge of the downs, at the top of Vicarage Farm, we had our eye on — and I said something about what a long walk it was for Walter, down the lane to those two tiny meadows, she looked up at Walter and said,

"If only you knew about the Secret of the Lane — what a treasure would be yours!"

I was there, but she seemed to be talking only to him. But she was a queer one, was Aunt Sarah."

"Yes," I said.

I could remember Aunt Sarah quite clearly, although she had died when I was only about eight or nine. She wasn't my aunt really; in fact, she was no relation at all. She was Uncle Walter's mother, and Uncle Walter was a relation only by marriage. He had married Aunt Maria, who was my mother's aunt and therefore my great-aunt.

Aunt Sarah's name was Mrs. Kennett. She lived in a cottage just around the first bend down Elderberry Lane — getting on for half-a-mile outside the village. It was rather a lonely place, but for that reason suited Aunt Sarah very well. She was an aloof person who, in village parlance, "kept herself to herself".

Aunt Sarah, as I remember her, was a stately person of rather above medium, height. When I saw her in chapel, three seats behind ours on the opposite side of the aisle, on Sunday evenings she was always immaculately dressed, generally in some frilly black material, with a black bonnet attached to her wavy grey hair by ornate hat-pins. She wore black gloves and almost always carried either an umbrella or parasol. She floated in, like some graceful sailing-craft, and perched herself, in a dignified posture, on the edge of the seat. I never saw her lean against the back of it. The service over, she was among the first to leave. Those whom she encountered on her way out she greeted with a quiet word and a smile, but she never joined the neighbourly groups who hung around for a Sabbath gossip in the porch or on the road outside. She never stayed for prayer-meetings or joined in open-air services, even when the band was playing.

Apart from Sundays, I sometimes saw her walking up to the village, to Mr. Jonas Nutbeam's shop, and in the holidays, when we catapult-armed boys were squolling the hedges for blackbirds or were playing fox-and-hounds over the fields, we would sometimes see her in the garden, attending to her washing. Then she wore a neat blouse and skirt and, more often than not, a white starched apron. Once or twice a year she walked the four miles to Wilcester to go shopping, sending back her parcels by carrier"s cart but herself walking home again.

She apparently had a reputation as a "wise woman" — what folklorists would call a "white witch", though I never heard the term used in Nadderbourne. I remember that once, when I had "pink-eye" (as conjunctivitis was then called), my mother sent my sister Emily down to Aunt Sarah "to see if she had anything for it", and Emily came back with a cooling herbal concoction which seemed to ease the inflammation. To enhance her resemblance to the traditional witch, she had a cat — not, it is true, a black one but a fine, glossy tortoiseshell.

Yes, I could accept Aunt Maria's dictum that she was a "a queer one". She didn't fit anywhere into the pattern of the ordinary village folk I knew, and she made no attempt to. In our flock of Rhode Island Red hens we had one Light Sussex, its white plumage conspicuous against the prevailing bronze-red. Aunt Sarah was like that.

I pedalled back up the hill to the farm, having forgotten to ask Aunt Maria about broody hens for my mother.

Chapter Two

On our Sunday afternoon walk Helen and I decided to check on the possibilities of treasure caches along Elderberry Lane. With Bouncer, my irrepressible mongrel terrier, in attendance we walked decorously past Aunt Maria's cottage, a good yard apart though prepared to close up as soon as we were beyond the range of prying eyes. Almost everyone in Nadderbourne went walking on fine Sunday afternoons in those days, the surrounding countryside offering four major alternative routes, of which Elderberry Lane was a favourite, except in high summer, when we preferred to stroll up Venables Drove to Nadderbourne Down, there to sit on the short, rabbit-nibbled turf and drink our fill of the satisfying panorama across the valley.

We had, of course, been familiar with all the local walks since infancy, and with Elderberry Lane in particular, for, being relatively level and surfaced with firm flints for its first mile or so, it had allowed our mothers to take us there for Sunday afternoon walks while we were still in our prams. Helen, whose father, Emmanuel Vicary, owned Glebe Farm, was as firmly rooted in Nadderbourne soil as I was, the Maidments and the Vicarys having farmed here for umpteen generations, to judge by the churchyard tombstones.

To an outside observer we would doubtless have appeared a couple of typical country innocents, as we sauntered along Elderberry Lane that Sunday afternoon, Helen in her demure brown Sunday dress and I in a purplish, double-breasted suit with fashionable Oxford bags, — a fashion I had seen on our French master just before I left High School in Wilcester two years earlier. But no such impartial observer was likely to see us. Such characters were rare in Nadderbourne in 1930.

16

With six hilly miles between our village and the city of Wilcester, Nadderbourne was still reserved almost exclusively for its own inhabitants, as it had always been during the twelve hundred years of its unrecorded history. What we had to be cautious about was observation by needle-eyed gossips, including Aunt Maria, who could be trusted to recount to the mothers of both of us anything she happened to see.

It was not to be supposed, of course, that the enigmatic treasure would reveal itself to us on a Sunday afternoon walk, when, with our best clothes on, we couldn't even dig if we found a likely spot. However, since I had retailed Aunt Maria's remarks to Helen we had both been exercising our minds about that treasure. Naturally we had known about Uncle Walter's treasure-hunting obsession since childhood; it was common knowledge and accepted as normal, like old hopping George's limp and the rector's habit of whistling his "s's". But now, with our interest reawakened, we had decided that we could at least size up the possibilities. Helen encouraged me. When I said, doubtfully,

"I don't suppose we can hope to notice anything that Uncle Walter hasn't, after all these years,"

She retorted,

"You never know. Every person sees a thing differently, so there's just a chance we shall spot something he hasn't".

At this juncture, therefore, I propose to invite the reader to accompany Helen and me along the tortuous, meandering lane, with a soft, south-west wind ruffling our hair and the song of skylarks and blackbirds providing a musical accompaniment. The attractive little map which Leslie Brook has drawn will supplement my efforts as a guide. As we start from the crossroads Nadderbourne village lies behind us, Aunt Maria's cottage on the bank on our left being the last in the village proper. We are walking eastwards, along the floor of the valley, with the towering scarp of Nadderbourne Down, then Addle Down, then, beyond the forest Juniper Down, three or four fields away to the right, and with the less spectacular Shuffley hills forming the northern horizon.

On our left, the road bank is three or four feet high, surmounted by a hedge. It appears that the lane has at some time been widened by cutting into the bank, but this must have been a long time ago, for the hedge is an ancient one. Six hundred years old, I would say, judging by its constituent bushes. One reckons a hundred years for each major species of bush, and these hedges have hawthorn, blackthorn, holly, maple, elder and a little oak. I have never been advised as to whether one counts in briars and brambles as well, but if so that would make them eight hundred years old.

The other side of the lane is level and has the wide grassy margin — as much as fifteen or twenty yards in places — which Uncle Walter finds so useful. The hedges at the back of the grass verge are solely of hawthorn and blackthorn, with a little hazel and masses of smothering traveller's joy ("bithywine" to us Nadderbourne natives). They evidently belong to the eighteenth century and were probably planted in the course of an enclosure in the 1780s. In 1930, the economic depression being at its nadir, nearly all the hedges are shaggy, overgrown and badly in need of the hedger's hook.

The fields on our right leading up to the foot of Nadderbourne Down, are known as Hodgkin's Fields, after some departed farmer, but the one nearest the corner, immediately opposite Uncle Walter's cottage, is, for some unknown reason, called Spallix. That is its name in the oldest maps of the parish. Perhaps it should be "Spallicks's", assuming that the field once belonged to a Mr. Spallick, but no-one knows.

On our left, the meadow atop the roadside bank, adjoining Uncle Walter's garden, bears the name of Halfpenny. Probably someone back in the Middle Ages paid a rent of a halfpenny for it. Here we pause to pick a bunch of scented violets for Helen , an accepted Nadderbourne tradition for those who take Sunday afternoon walks in March. The violets come in three colours, — purple, white and a dull magenta-pink, the last being rare. In the deep shade beneath some of the oak scrub are moschatel flowers, their little green heads facing four ways, like a town hall clock. I start to pick some of these for Helen, as they are about the same size as violets, but she says No, they would take the scent away from the violets. I don't know whether they do or not, but they have a distinct scent of musk.

"I've found a treasure!" I explained, and pulled back some trailing ivy from a thorn bush to reveal to Helen a hedge-sparrow's nest with three turquoise-blue eggs. The first of the season.

After she has clambered up the bank to inspect it and jumped down again, she muses.

"I wonder about this bank. Do you think anybody has ever buried a treasure here?"

"They could have," I admit. "But why should they?"

Then I remember that when I was a very small boy and heard my father talking about taking money to the bank I used to wonder why he bothered to go to Wilcester when there was a perfectly adequate bank at the back of our cowshed.

"I suppose there might be some simple old chap who thought the same," I say, after we had laughed about the fancy.

"Even if there was," points out Helen, "he surely wouldn't do it here, by a public road? He'd dig a hole in a bank in his garden."

The logic seems unanswerable.

We saunter on, past the entrance to Venables' Drove, which leads to the downs but where puddles of water still lie in deep ruts, and come up to the bend in the road where Noah's Close is on one hand and Austin's on the other. Noah's Close was named after a man, a smallholder, whom my father could remember, and he assumed that Austin was another long-dead proprietor. In the corner of Austin's stands a giant maple-tree, its trunk now riddled with holes, in which jackdaws and stock doves nest. This afternoon a little owl is yelping in the lower branches on the far side, so I lead Helen around to the far side, on the pretext of seeing whether it is occupying one of the nesting holes. Hidden by the trunk from the road and from the other quarters by hedges, I snatch the opportunity to slip my arm around her waist and kiss her. It has happened before at this spot, so she knew what to expect.

The owl ceases yelping and flies away, but the sound of children's voices approaching along the lane makes us break up our embrace. That is another hazard for courting couples walking out on Sunday afternoons. They can be reasonably sure of meeting families or parts of families spaced at quarter-mile intervals. The approaching detachment consists of the majority of the Bead family — Susan and her five children, two of them in a push-chair. Her husband, Cliff, is Farmer Gutteridge's dairyman and will be milking at this hour.

Having regained the road and resumed our decorous parade, we exchange greetings with the Beads, by which time we have reached the ruins of Sarah Kennett's cottage, with Ensell's Garden on the opposite side of the lane. Ensell's Garden is a garden no longer but a cow paddock, and no-one in Nadderbourne remembers who Ensell was, though the name still sticks.

Sarah's cottage was the scene of Nadderbourne's greatest tragedy, the details of which I offer later. The events are still sufficiently recent for the cottage to be relatively sound, though the thatched roof has sagged into great holes, allowing rain to soak the bedroom ceilings and cause them too to collapse. Stains discolour the interior walls, where thatch-impregnated water has trickled down, and the doors no longer fit cleanly into their warped frames. The place is not quite past repair but, deteriorating at the present rate, it will be after the storms of a few more winters. And no-one, of course, is going to repair it, after what had happened there.

We push past the broken gate into the garden and pick a few snowdrops that still manage to flourish under Aunt Sarah's cob-nut bush and around the old well-crib, but we do not enter the house. That would be asking for trouble in broad daylight, with villagers passing along the lane at intervals of about a quarter-of-an-hour.

Someone would be sure to see us and report to someone else who would tell our parents. We can afford to wait till dark evenings, when the only danger of interruption comes from other couples — for the amenities of Sarah's cottage are widely appreciated. Time is constantly remoulding attitudes. It was not many years earlier that I, with Billy Davis, Stan Moxam, Ted Vicary and the other boys, would march boldly in on stormy afternoons, to spend a few hours of target practice with our air-guns. When the local birds became too wary to venture within range of artillery mounted in the cottage windows we pencilled pictures of elephants, giraffes, polar bears and other animals on the plaster walls and shot darts into them. (The pictures remained till the house eventually disintegrated.) Alas, that with adolescence the age of innocence recedes. Now I only enter the cottage furtively — "in the twilight, in the evening, in the black and dark night", as the Book of Proverbs puts it. Still, it is even more fun.

"Could there be any treasure buried here?" Helen pondered.

"I shouldn't think so. If Aunt Sarah had the treasure she would have given it to Uncle Walter, not buried it, wouldn't she?"

"I don't know. Look at it this way. She knows about this treasure. She knows where it is. She talks about it, though admittedly not much. But she doesn't give it to Uncle Walter. And she doesn't tell him where to look. Does she want to find it for himself?"

We rack our brains in vain for an answer.

"Perhaps," suggests Helen, dubiously, " perhaps it's treasure with a curse. I've read stories where someone has hidden a treasure and put a spell on it."

"It could be," I agree, slowly. "If Aunt Sarah knew about such a treasure she would, in one way, want Uncle Walter to have it and, in another, would be afraid it would bring him bad luck. So she would just drop hints."

"Was Aunt Sarah superstitious?"

"No," I say thoughtfully. "I wouldn't say she was."

So the riddle remains as far from a solution as ever. We gaze at the cottage, remembering well the details of its interior architecture and knowing that there is nothing there, in the matter of bread-ovens and cupboards, that has escaped our previous attentions. We look reflectively at the old well, but my father, whose land adjoins Sarah's garden, has nailed down the lid, for fear that someone would leave it open and give one of the sheep the opportunity of falling in. Then, hearing more voices down the lane, we hurry out of the garden and resume our innocent walk.

On our left now lies the field known as Glebe Land, which was once evidently Church property and which is now part of Mr. Vicary's Glebe Farm. On our right a large field named Stony Lawn, on the surface of which large flint stones are certainly plentiful, extends towards the downs. Between the field and the hill slope, however, is another enclosure called Ship Pennings, which name puzzled me for a long time until I realised that "ship" is simply the local pronunciation of "sheep". I noticed that our shepherd, Tom Glasbury, would cut his syllables short, saying, for instance,

"Don't ee bring thik thur gurt camel of a hoss anywhere nigh thik hay-rick. I da want all on't vor the ship."

He is great at ensuring there is plenty of food for his sheep, no matter what other farm animals go short.

The approaching voices belong to Mrs. Abbott and her daughter Freda, now married to Fred Darby, the bus driver. They are pushing Freda's new baby, Rita, in an imposing pram. Dan Abbott, who has allowed his wife to wear the breeches for too long to hope for any respite, shambles along ten yards in the rear, his cream-coloured lurcher, Major, accompanying him with a similar cowed expression. He grabs his collar, as I grab Bouncer's, to forestall a fracas.

We stop for a moment to allow Helen, her feminine instincts aroused, to admire the baby, while Dan and Major hang back and pretend to be interested in a mole-hill. Then, with the usual polite nothings, we pass on, towards the forest that looms just ahead.

Just before one reaches the keeper's cottage, where at this time Henry Upshot is living, there is, on the same side of the road, a pond, partly in the field called Vincent's and partly on the common strip that is the roadside verge. This road Uncle Walter finds providential, for it provides his cows with a good drink at a half-way stage and absolves him from the necessity of installing a water-supply in his meadows. (Not, of course, that he would have done; the cows would have had to go thirsty.) A sagging wire fence across the middle of the pond marks the boundary between the field and the road. The water is black and looks unappetising, but a straggling bramble on the field side offers a little cover and is in some years occupied by a nesting moorhen. Migrating birds, such as warblers and wagtails, and downland birds, such as peewits and stone curlew, also drop in to quench their thirst. White Ox Pond is the local name, and it is easy to imagine why it should be termed an ox pond, — though why a particular white ox should be referred to seems inexplicable.

No birds are visible this afternoon, probably because the pedestrian traffic has frightened them away, but stooping down, we find frog spawn floating at the edge of the pond. Then Helen has an inspiration.

"Supposing the treasure's at the bottom of the pond!" she suggests.

"Like the Wiltshire Moonrakers," she continues. It is certainly worth considering. We both know the story of the Wiltshire Moonrakers, of course. In smuggling days two Wiltshire countrymen on a moonlit night were conveying a load of contraband brandy along a road near Devizes when they heard approaching hooves which they rightly surmised told of the imminent appearance of excise-men. They had to hurry to get the brandy kegs out of the cart and into a roadside pond, which seemed to be the only possible hiding-place, before the horsemen appeared. Though suspicious, the customs officers saw only a couple of simple-looking yokels with an empty cart, so, with a brief word, they passed on. Whereupon the two smugglers, pulling out rakes from under the cart, set about raking the kegs out of the pond.

So engrossed were they in their work that they failed to hear the return of the excise men, silent because they were trotting their horses on grass. The shock they had when they looked up and saw they had spectators is easily imagined. Their reaction says much for their presence of mind.

"Rake away, neighbour," muttered one.

"What do you think you're up to?" demanded a customs officer.

"We be atter thik gurt cheese," the spokesman for the guilty pair informed him. "Don't ee see en, mister? He's a-fallen in the pond, and we be gwaine to git en out.."

The exise men stared at the reflection of the moon in the pond; then exploded in guffaws of laughter. Off they rode, to tell their mates of the two witless, drunken Wiltshiremen whom they found raking a pond "for the shadder of the moon."

Left in peace, the two yokels retrieved their brandy. There could certainly be an analogy here at White Ox Pond, I concede. A pond could be a useful place to hide treasure. Then I remember.

"The pond went dry in the dry summer of 1921," I say. "My father often talks about that year, and I can just remember it."

"Well, the treasure could have been put there long ago, and the pond made afterwards," suggests Helen, reluctant to abandon her theory. "The treasure would be buried in the ground at the bottom of the pond, so you wouldn't see it, even when the pond dried out."

It is possible, I suppose.

"But, if so, how would Aunt Sarah know about it?" I ask. "Aunt Sarah and nobody else."

It opens the door to conjecture. Perhaps Aunt Sarah, out walking at night, had seen the deed being done. The treasure would in that case be stolen property, and Aunt Sarah would have natural hesitations about telling her son, lest he should find it and then be disappointed at having to surrender it. But no, that was nonsense. Aunt Sarah was a rigidly upright lady. If she had seen any such nefarious activities she would surely have informed the police. And what were her actual words? —

"If only you knew the Secret of the Lane — what a treasure would be yours!"

That seemed to say that if Uncle Walter found the treasure he would be allowed to keep it. Everything is as puzzling as ever. Helen pushes aside my arm, which has somehow become linked with hers while we are standing speculating about the pond, and we resume our walk, a yard apart. We are about to pass the keeper's cottage, and Mrs. Upshot may be looking out of the front window.

The keeper's cottage is tucked into a shadowy corner just outside the limits of the Forest of Princedun. It is a single-storied building, its thatched roof having scalloped edges like an umbrella. Two rustic poles support a thatched porch, and the windows are diamond-paned. The ground plan is completely circular. The cottage could have taken its place without question in any fairy story by Grimm or Andersen. The Seven Dwarfs would have been perfectly at home in it.

Here dwells the unpopular Henry Upshot, as did his father, Adam

Upshot, before him. They came from Gloucestershire when the old Earl of Crewkerne married Lady Emma Battesley, whose father, the Earl of Yarlington, was a Gloucestershire landowner. The Upshots were retainers of sorts of the Yarlington family. The cottage resembles a military outpost on the edge of enemy territory. Here, as the Roman legions in times past kept a watch on the barbarians on the other side of the Rhine, so Henry and his predecessors have kept an eye on the incorrigible poachers of Nadderbourne. He and the villagers watch each other with mutual suspicion. The ceaseless though usually veiled hostility has stamped its mark on Henry's character. He is a swarthy, taciturn man, with dark, southern eyes. Gipsy blood, says my father, and mutters something about "setting a thief to catch a thief".

"If anything was buried in the pond," points our Helen, "the keeper ought to have seen it. I wonder how long ago it happened."

"If it ever did," I corrected her.

But we agree that, if the Secret of the Lane lay here, it is likely that the keeper, whoever it might be was occupying the cottage at that time, would know something about it.

"We must ask our fathers who was living here in the old days," we say.

Past the keeper's cottage Elderberry Lane swerves to the left, northwards, to skirt the edge of Princedun Forest. That is a predictable arrangement, for the Forest comprises the remnants of an ancient Royal Chase, preserved for deer throughout the Middle Ages. A deep ditch, with accompanying earth bank, still marks its boundaries for several miles. Perhaps in times past a fence surmounted the bank. Anyhow, the Forest is strictly preserved, as strictly for pheasants now as for deer in the past, and the peasantry housed in the neighbouring villages are required to keep their distance. In the lifetime of the old Earl of Crewkerne the regulations had been relaxed to the extent that the keepers had instructions not to interfere with women and children using the woodland paths for obviously innocent purposes, such as picking primroses, but with the accession of the young Earl (now, incidentally, a man in his fifties) the old rigid regime has been re-applied. As already mentioned, much of Henry Upshot's current unpopularity has resulted from his ordering out of the woods some villagers picking flowers. His action was strongly resented, and Henry, rather than the remote Earl, has all the blame.

A hundred yards or so past his house an old woodland track leads off into the forest. It was here that the encounter between Henry and the women had taken place, for that section of the forest, known as Hobbit's Copse, is the nearest and most easily accessible for the housewives of Nadderbourne. Now a recently erected five-barred gate, padlocked and reinforced by barbed wire along the top and barbed wire fences on either side, bars the way. "Trespassers will be Prosecuted" proclaims a bold notice, in black lettering on white board, nailed to the gate. The track on the far side is reported to lead eventually to Princedun House, though doubtless it loses its identity in the maze of other tracks which transected the forest. Neither Helen nor I have ever trodden it.

Peeping through the gate, we can see roseattes of early primroses, motionless and colourful as those dome-shaped glass paper-weights, pinning the carpet of dead leaves to the damp soil beneath the hazels. Ethereal anemones, light as thistledown, bow their heads in acknowledgment of the radiance of the sinking sun.

The temptation to trespass to complete our posy of wild flowers is easily resisted through the knowledge that we will be able to pick all we want on the edge of the woods farther along the lane. So we saunter on, with the forest on our right and a series of fields sloping away to the low hills on our left.

The first of these is Wells Piece. Repeating the name sends us speculating again about its meaning, for if real wells were referred to, that suggests other possible hiding-places. On the other hand, the field might have belonged to a man named Wells. We make a note to find out.

Then come Grove End Fields, which are the last ones on our farm. In a corner by the lane stand several straw-ricks, which I helped to make at threshing-time back in October and which now have an overwhelming fascination for me as representing the World, the Flesh and the Devil. For, miscalculating the quantity of straw available, we had some to spare and so had to make a small rick as a kind of annex to a larger one. Seeking shelter from a storm one afternoon, soon afterwards, I discovered that it is easy to tunnel along the joint between the two ricks. One can pull out the straw by armfuls and yet leave a weatherproof roof overhead. Moreover, the entrance can easily be camoflaged. So, inside I constructed a snug little nest, to which, in due course, I introduced a hesitant Helen.

It is towards this haven that I now tentatively make my way. I was never one to miss an opportunity. But Helen, wiser than I, decides otherwise.

"No Steve. Not this afternoon", she says urgently, hanging back. "you know what a lot of people come along here on a Sunday afternoon. What if somebody came just as we were crawling out! And what is my mother going to say if she finds straw on my best dress?"

These are cogent arguments, which I have to accept.

"Very well. But tonight , then."

"We'll see," says Helen.

The next field to Grove End is a triangular one known, for some unexplained reason, as Nimitty. It has a grove of yew trees at the far corner, probably a relic of a larger wood. Then, on the other side of a lane called Adam's Drove, is a large field, White Ox Acres. Goodness knows why the White Ox should appear again. At the far end of it are three barrows, or tumuli, the tallest of which is known to us as Golden Cap Tump. Some of the very old folk used to say that you could see a man with a golden cap walking about there on Midsummer Night and other special dates.

By this time we are becoming rather bored with Uncle Walter's treasure, but the tumuli set us conjecturing again. They seem the obvious place for buried treasure. But doubtless Uncle Walter thought of that long ago, and what would Aunt Sarah know of any treasure buried in a barrow.

Meantime, the forest of Princedun spreads its tree canopy over the deer leap and the margins of the land on the opposite side. The section of the wood here is known as Verngrove. On the woodland banks we pick as many primroses as Helen feels she needs, and find, to her delight, two or three specimens of the rare, parasitic toothwort, which is about as attractive as a dead wallflower. There are more sweet-scented violets here, too, and myriads of small black wolf-spiders scurrying about in the sun.

Eventually we reach the end of the forest, on rising ground where the woodland merges with the downland. Juniper Down is an obvious name for this waste, for numerous prickly juniper bushes stud it, like hiles of sheaves in a harvest field. As we knew would happen, when we round the corner and come in view of the down multitudes of rabbits dart for their burrows, then stand for a moment, surveying us before diving into oblivion. The holes are numerous enough to resemble shell and shrapnel holes on a battle-field, and the predominant colour of the field is grey with exposed earth, rather than the green of the meadows nearer Nadderbourne. In the distance, over the receding frontier of the forest, a buzzard, a bird rarer than it might have been were it not for the zealous work of Henry Upshot with his twelve-bore shotgun, is circling on rounded, uptilted wings, deciding which young rabbit to dine upon.

With White Ox Acres still on our left, and on the crest of the hill, we come at last to Uncle Walter's two meadows, elliptical enclosures obviously carved at some time out of waste land bordering the lane. They are reasonably green, due to a barrier of wire netting which Uncle Walter, with untypical enterprise, has erected around them. His efforts were motivated not so much by a determination to conserve the grass for his cows as by a desire to catch rabbits. At a score or two of intervals around the perimeter the wire has been lifted to allow access to venturesome rabbits, and in each place Uncle Walter has either a gin-trap or a wire snare. Rabbits are an important item in his income.

We spot Uncle Walter kneeling by a hedge on the far side of the first meadow, adjusting a wire snare. He waves vaguely when we hail him but makes no attempt to come over to talk. Uncle Walter is an introvert type, content with his own company. So we leave him to it.

We stand on the crest of Dane Hill, leading down steeply to the old stone bridge, Puck Bridge, over the Coxenbourne. The brook marks the boundary between our parish and Avonchurch, and, as a matter of fact, the last section of Elderberry Lane, after it reached the forest, is alternatively known as Avonchurch Lane. The sallow catkins down by the stream are golden with pollen, and somewhere in the willow thicket a chiffchaff, the first of the spring, is calling. By a pool near the willows we can see the glittering gold of a clump of marsh marigold, and more are visible farther upstream, in the meadow known as the Slob.

Helen's instincts tell her to hurry down the hill to pick some, but I point out that (a) she is already carrying as many flowers as she can hold and (b) it is getting on for tea-time. The second argument is the deciding one, for Helen's mother is a woman of routine, who likes to see her family gathered around the meal table together and in good time — or awkward questions are asked.

So we turn round and retrace our steps towards Nadderbourne. This time, though, I slip my arm around Helen's waist, and she responds by curving hers around mine and anchoring her fingers to my right-hand pocket. We guess we will be reasonably safe from observation, for by this time the promenading families of Nadderbourne will be nearing home and, anyway, none had been in sight as we gazed along the lane towards Avonchurch. There is only Uncle Walter, who can be relied upon to notice nothing or, if by any chance he does, will not think it of sufficient interest to tell Aunt Maria. If she had no-one but Uncle Walter for company, Aunt Maria would have a lonely life.

Chapter Three

It would be a mistake to suppose that probing the secret of the lane became as much an obsession with us as with Uncle Walter. We dug into it by fits and starts. Now and again, when I was alone in the field, I tried to analyse the numerous possibilities, but without much progress.

April was a busy month. Rain in March had prevented us from finishing the barley sowing, which consequently kept us occupied till the middle of April and caused the sowing of vegetables to fall into arrears. Then in the latter part of the month the evenings were devoted to practising at the nets and preparing the ground for the cricket season, the first match impending on the first week-end of May.

At the end of April Helen caught mumps and was confined to her house for a week or so. My young brothers and sisters confidently predicted that I would catch it, too, and, to their delight, they were right. Instead of playing in that first cricket match, against our ancient enemies from Avonchurch, I curled up dolefully in bed, my temperature soaring like a broody hen's and my face resembling a blown-up pig's bladder.

Knowing that by this time Helen must be well on the way to recovery, I asked my mother if she could come up and sit by my sickbed.

"No, she can not," declared my mother, a stickler for the proprieties.

I tried again a few days later, when I was downstairs, luxuriating in an armchair by a log fire. My mother didn't reply, but the next afternoon she showed Helen into the parlour. I guess she had a word with Mrs. Vicary.

When she had left the room, Helen came and sat on the arm of my chair, and minutes passed. It was perhaps an hour later when, other topics of conversation temporarily exhausted, we started to talk to Uncle Walter, Aunt Maria and the secret of the lane.

"It seems to me," said Helen, "that we have to start with your Aunt Sarah, — Mrs. Kennett. She was the only one who ever said anything about a secret."

"That's true," I agreed.

"So she knew something that nobody else did. How did she come to know?"

"Well, living alone in that cottage down the lane, she would have a better chance than anyone else of seeing what went on down there."

"I think," said Helen, falling back on her feminine intuition," that the key to the secret is in Aunt Sarah herself. So I've been asking myself what we know about her. I've been asking my mother, too."

A picture of that stately, immaculate lady, still handsome in her old age, flashed through my mind. She was a minor figure in the background of my early boyhood. I could not claim to know anything about her at all, except, of course, about the manner of her death. That could never be forgotten.

I must have been about eight when it happened. There was, I remember, a tremendous stir — more policemen and other strangers about the village than we had ever seen before or since. My parents tried to keep me away from the cottage, but, of course, after school I crept down through the meadows with the other boys and peeped through the hedge, trying to see what was going on.

In retrospect, the story was fairly straightforward though gruesome.

Soon after I started school a big boy came to live with the Upshots, the keepers. His name was Isaac Melkin. We called him Big Izzie. He was a lout of a boy, with a big head as round as a football, close-cropped ginger hair, ears sticking out like jug-handles, pug nose, hardly any neck, and a body like a fat pig's. The information current in the village was that he was a grandson of old Adam Upshot, who was then alive, and therefore nephew of Henry. We little kids were a bit overawed by his size at first, but we soon learned his weakness. He was strong, but clumsy, and he couldn't run very fast.

He left school when he was fourteen and went to work on Thomas Laversuch's farm. One Sunday evening he lifted the latch and entered Sarah Kennett's cottage. The old lady was sitting in her high-backed chair, watching the fire. He crept up behind her and hit her on the head with a rusty plough-spanner. She fell forward on the hearth, and he hit her several more times more, to make sure.

Then he started back to ransack the house, looking for money. Leaving the clammy spanner on the floor, where he had dropped it. He searched in the tea caddy and ornaments on the mantelpiece, in the old cupboard by the grate, in the dresser drawers. There he found four pounds and some small change in a tin box.

Evidently disappointed, he went upstairs. Sarah had a candle in a blue-enamelled candlestick, ready to light her to bed. He struck a match, fumbling over the task through still having his gloves on, let the wick clear and went to the stair door. The winding stairs would have creaked loudly under his weight. I guess he must have been sweating.

In the bedroom he faced a rickety chest of drawers supporting a looking-glass and a brush-and comb set, both brush and comb fuzzy with grey hairs, like those sticking to the plough-spanner. The mirror reflected from the opposite wall a picture of a lighthouse on a rock. He started, dazedly, to try to decipher the accompanying religious text, being able to read only with difficulty, when the room was suddenly filled with spitting fury. From the bed, where she had been curled up asleep, the cat, startled, hurled herself across the room and bashed herself against the closed window. Baffled and dazed, she ricochetted across the chest of drawers, knocking brush, comb, mirror and ornaments to the floor, then made another attempt at the window. Izzie instinctively moved across to the window, to open it so that she could escape, whereupon the hysterical cat launched herself at his face.

The smarting pain sent him reeling back. Protecting his eyes with one gloved hand, he endeavoured to grapple with the furious animal with the other. For a few moments the room whirled with the wild melee. Then it was over. He had been able to get a lucky grip on the desperate, clawing cat and had hurled her, squawling, against the wall.

The story now takes a bizarre turn, which perhaps illustrates the abnormality of Izzie, though perhaps what he did was a natural reaction. Who knows what we would do in such a situation?

Breathing heavily and with blood trickling from the red furrows down his cheeks, he pounced in panic anger on the temporarily winded cat.

"I'll larn ee! I'll show ee, you bloody moggie!"

His groping free hand felt his dangling tie, which his aunt insisted he wore on Sundays. It would serve as well as anything. Tearing it off, he tied a slip-knot and looped it around the cat's neck. The room was not big enough to swing a cat in, or he would have taken a savage delight in doing so. Instead, he stumbled downstairs, dangling the cat and giving it a gratuitous thump or two against the walls as he went. He had noticed several large, blacksmith-made nails, for hanging ham and herbs, in the exposed beams of the living-rooom. From one of these he hanged the cat.

He stood back to survey his work. The cat seemed limp and dead. He hoped it was not, so that it could wriggle and squirm and feel itself slowly strangling. But it did not give him the satisfaction of a single twitch. So, with a final oath, he turned and went upstairs to resume his search.

It was fruitless. He probed into every corner of both little bedrooms without finding a hint of cash. He even pulled up one or two floor-boards and turned the mattress upside down. There was nothing anywhere.

It must be downstairs, in some hiding-place he had missed, he decided. So down the winding wooden stairs he stumbled. Looking around to decide where to resume his search, he became vaguely aware of something missing. Suddenly, he knew what it was. The cat had gone.

The discovery filled him with a sense of menace. He moved

restlessly around the tiny rooms, uncertain whether to concentrate on finding the cash or the cat. The door creaked. The hair bristled on his nape, and he dived for his weapon, the plough-spanner. But no-one came in. He realised he must have left the door unlatched and that the rising wind had pushed it open.

So, with the door open, the cat would have been able to creep out, — assuming, that is, that it could somehow have wriggled out of its noose. He went to the door and peered into the night, palely illuminated by the crisp, glinting, metallic light of a waning moon. He saw the cat standing in the middle of the garden path, by the cabbages. By a trick of the moonlight, she looked twice her normal size....and from her neck still dangled his noose.

The sense of imminent danger shook him. His cunning little brain had thought out answers to the obvious hazards. He had worn gloves. The ground was dry, so he had left no muddy footprints. There was nothing to associate him, in anyone's mind, with the blood-stained spanner. He had already planned, in any case, to set fire to the cottage, to destroy any possible evidence. No doubt he could think of some explanation for the scratches on his face. But of what use was all this if the cat were found with his tie around her neck?

He advanced a few cautious paces and raised his hand. The cat stood glaring at him. She waited until the spanner was flying through the air before she leapt aside and streaked for the nearest tree — a towering, ancient fir which then leaned over the garden. (It was blown down in a gale some four or five years later.) The spanner bounced from the path where she had been standing, hit a pile of unsawn logs under the tree and dropped to the ground.

Izzie ran forward and peered up through the shaggy branches of the fir. The cat he could see quite plainly against the pewter-black sky. Clinging defiantly to the tree, she spat a challenge down at him. Fortunately fir trees, having plenty of cross branches, are easy enough to climb. The wood-pile around the trunk gave him a good start.

Slowly they both clambered upwards. Izzie, despite his weight, wasn't bad at climbing trees, and, desperate though he was to catch that cat, he was careful not to put a foot wrong. Whenever he raised his eyes they caught the fixed, baleful glare of the cat's glittering in the moonlight and seeming never to move from his. There was presently nothing in the world but the cat and himself and the rough, sticky bark and needles of the fir, all swaying in a macabre harmony with the clouds and the buoyant moon.

The cat had made a mistake at last. She had moved out from the trunk along one of the branches. It was bending beneath her clutching weight. Izzie, below her, estimated that if he too moved outwards along the branch on which he was standing he would be able to reach up and grab her. Carefully he edged along, balancing himself with the aid of another branch at throat level. The cat had evidently realised her error and was looking round frantically for a way of escape.

Suddenly she sprang. Straight at his head. He leaned back involuntarily, raising one arm to shield his eyes and swinging his weight away from the menace. Unequal to the sudden stress, the branch snapped with a pistol-like crack. For a moment he hung, snatching desperately at the jagged twigs and prickly foliage. Then the branches in his hands also gave way and he plunged, doomed as Lucifer, down the dark funnel of the night.

He felt the explosion of pain as his body crashed against the woodpile, but he never knew that, when he finally crumpled on the garden in the moonbeams, his bloodied head rested upon a bloody spanner.

Indoors, the cat crept to the hearth rug and curled up on the old lady's skirts, in front of the dying fire.

And, how the reader may well ask, do we know all these harrowing details, seeing that there were no witnesses? Well, reconstruction of the tragedy was a favourite occupation in Nadderbourne for weeks after the event. The police did it, the doctor did it, the reporters did it, and the villagers of Nadderbourne, whose experience at minding their neighbours' business has long been unsurpassed, did it. The above account, as a matter of fact, is substantially that which appeared in the Wilcester Guardian and South Markshire Gazette in the week following the coroner's inquest, with certain embellishments gleaned from local sources.

Nor were the Nadderbournians at a loss for a motive for Izzie's assault. Mrs. Vicary said that Mrs. Stout had told her that on the previous Friday evening she had been in the shop when Mrs. Burkett and Mrs. Hardicott had been talking about Sarah Kennett and that she, Mrs. Stout, had noticed Izzie there, waiting his turn to be served. The conversation had drifted to Old Moll Hart, a local witch of a bygone age who had, it was said, the ability to turn herself into a hare.

"A witch she were, Mabel. The last of 'em, so 'twere said ... but it's my belief we got another down Elderberry Lane."

"You think so, Mrs. Burkett?"

"Ah, I do. And I'm not the only one, either. When you come to think of it, there's thik old woman, living there, all alone, right outside the village, and with pots of money hidden about the house. You wouldn't say 'twas safe, now would you? But 'tis as safe as if 'twere all in the bank. 'Cos who do you think would go out there at dead of night to rob her? Eh?"

"Nobody round these parts, Mrs. Burkett. Of that I'm sure."

"No, nobody round these parts. They'd be all as scared as sparrows in a trap, for all there must be a hundred pounds and more in that house if there's a penny...I'd stake this yer basket of groceries on that."

"Is there anything more, Mrs. Burkett?"

"No, that's the lot, Olive...Oh, I see you've got some birthday cards. It's my Julie's twenty-third Monday. Perhaps I'd better send her one. All right, Olive. Just serve Mrs. Hardicott, while I choose one."

"How about you, Izzie? You don't want much, I suppose?"

"No. Thank you, Mrs. Hardicott... only a packet of fags for my uncle. That's the sort, Olive. Ta."

Such was the crucial conversation, as remembered by the participants and bandied back and forth around the village. Mrs. Burkett, a notorious gossip, came in for criticism from many who were no better themselves, but no-one doubted that the talk of a hundred pounds hidden in the cottage had been sufficient to tempt Izzie.

So that was the tragic end of this dignified old lady, murdered by an oaf for her money.

But what was her beginning?

On this matter we had far less information, but Helen had been tactfully questioning her mother and had gleaned the following facts.

Sarah Kennett had arrived in Nadderbourne in 1867 or thereabouts, as a young widow with a baby, Uncle Walter. Her husband, she said, was a sailor who had been drowned, and she was still wearing widow's weeds. The cottage down Elderberry Lane, where she made her home, belonged then to the Princedun estate, and it was understood that she was given tenancy through the good offices of the agent, a Mr. Oldcastle. After her death it was learned that at some time she had purchased the freehold, so it passed to Uncle Walter.

That seemed to sum up her life history. Mrs. Vicary surmised that she must have been about twenty when she came to live in Nadderbourne, so she could have been married for only a short time before she was made a widow. Where she came from, nobody knew. She never had relatives to visit her and never went away visiting. When she died, no-one from outside Nadderbourne came to the funeral, though the story received wide publicity.

"What was she like?" Helen asked her mother, who had replied, "I really can't say. I never got to know her well. But nobody did. She was that kind of woman."

Which was much the same as my mother had told me. Aunt Sarah remained an enigma. Any possibility of unravelling the Secret of the Lane by studying her seemed to be blocked. Although there might have been a mystery about her origins, on the other hand there might have been none; it was all so long ago. And, after living at Nadderbourne for over fifty years, whatever may have happened before she came there could hardly have counted for much at the end.

I did, however, come upon one other item of information about Aunt Sarah's character, rather surprisingly, when I was convalescing from mumps. I walked out into the bright May sunshine, inspected the vegetable garden and then sauntered over to where old Eli Hemmings was thatching the calf-shed. Eli, who never minded breaking off for a yarn, came down the ladder and refreshed himself with cider from a plough-bottle. We chatted of this and that, and then it occurred to me to bring up the subject of Aunt Sarah. She would be only about ten years younger than she was so should remember her well.

"Ah, I knew her. I knew her, " he averred. "A fine woman."

"She seems quite good-looking from her photo," I prompted.

"Ah, she were that. A proper good-looker."

"Mum says she was a rather reserved person. It was hard to get to know her."

"Mebbe. But she didn't get on too well with women. Didn't have much time for 'em. She was a man's woman."

"Was she, now? But she was a widow."

"From choice, me lad. From choice. She could have had her pick from any of a number of lads of her own age round her. I used to watch 'em trying to make up to 'er. There were Ennery Spry and Dick Erris, ... oh, and Matthew Vicary ... aye, he made a real set at her. But she oodn't have none of 'em. 'Oodn't give 'em no encouragement at all."

"No?"

"No. Not a bit. Mind you, that were why the oomen didn't take to her. Oomen can sense competition a mile off, and it gets their hackles up. But, as it turned out, they was wasting their time being jealous about Sarah Kennett. 'Tis a bit surprisin', though. She ought to have got married agen. She were a man's ooman."

Chapter Four

When, about a week before haymaking, Helen said one evening,
    "Hey, Steve, I think I've got another clue,"
    I had to ask her what in the world she was talking about. Life had
been so full that I had for the time forgotten about Uncle Walter's
secret treasure. One day when I had been rolling a barley-field with a
horse-roller all day and was complaining about feeling tired (for we
had no tractors in Nadderbourne in 1930), my father had promised me
that after harvest, if it was a good harvest, he was going to buy a new
car and I could have the old Ford 8. So, anticipating the time when I
would be an owner-driver, I had taken to borrowing the car any
evening I could and getting in some practice. I was also teaching Helen
to drive, among other things
    Still, the Secret of the Lane was there in the background, obtrud-
ing from time to time as if to challenge me to solve it, and here it was,
cropping up again.
    "I've been talking to my Grandmother, " said Helen. "She's not
all that much younger than Mrs. Kennett was, and she can remember
her well. And when I asked her what sort of woman she was, she said
she was a strange one. She said,
    "Do you know, she used to go walking up in Princedun Woods on
moonlight nights, dressed in her best clothes and carrying a parasol"
    "What was she doing, Gran?" I asked, and she said,
    "I think she was gathering herbs. She showed me some once, which
she said had to be gathered at full moon, when the dew was on them.
Ah, she was a strange one,"
    What do you think, Steve? Does that give us a lead?"

"It could do, I suppose," I surmised. "Aunt Sarah knew a lot about herbs. My mum used to send down to her for some sort or other of tonic for me and the other kids when we were ill."

"My mum did for me, too. Steve, don't you think that perhaps Aunt Sarah discovered some very rare and valuable herb down Elderberry Lane? If it were found there and nowhere else, it could be worth a lot of money. That could be the secret of the lane."

"I suppose it could," I conceded, doubtfully, "But I've been going up and down that lane all my life, and I've never seen anything unusual."

"That's because you haven't known what to look for. You wouldn't know a rare herb if somebody picked it and stuffed it under you nose."

"Neither would you. Look, here's one...see if you can recognise that."

"Aoow, you beast...it's a stinging nettle; Ooooooh!"

After an interlude of horse-play, we resumed the conversation.

"The thing to do is to ask an expert," declared Helen. "I know. I'll ask Miss Simpkins."

Miss Annabella Simpkins had been infant's teacher, in charge of the "little room" at Nadderbourne School when we were both pupils there. The daughter of a former farmer of Nadderbourne, she represented rural gentility. Now retired, she lived in a house ("The Willow") and on a small pension left her by her father, spending her time on such feminine pastimes as embroidery and pressing flowers and always lending her support to worthy causes. Almost certainly she would profess knowledge of herbs, even if she knew little about them. And probably she would have books on the subject.

Driving the car for pleasure on Sunday was taboo — indeed, I knew better that to suggest it. So the next Sunday afternoon saw us taking our usual walk down Elderberry Lane. Helen had already reported to me on her visit to Miss Simpkins, who had been flattered that a young girl should come to her as an expert. She proved to know very little about herbs but had lent Helen some books, which however, had shown themselves to be somewhat indigestible.

One was Anne Pratt's *Flowering Plants of Great Britain*, 1899 edition, but it was in four hefty volumes. Although it was generously illustrated, searching for the scraps of information that we wanted was like looking for a grain of wheat in a bushel of flour.

We took a few random samples. Concerning Catmint we read:

> It is sometimes used medicinally; and the leaves of several foreign species are eaten in order to restore tone to the digestive organs. Commercon states that a species common in Madagascar, which has tubular roots, is a favourite vegetable; the roots are called *Houmines*. Hoffman relates that the root of our native Cat-mint, if chewed, will make the most gentle persons fierce and wrathful, and adds that Turneiserius tells of a hangman who was usually gentle and pusillanimous, and who never had courage to perform the duties of his wretched vocation until he had first prepared himself by masticating this root. The writer of these pages, who, with a friend who joined in the experiment, chewed a piece of this bitter and aromatic substance, of the length of a finger, is able, however, to assure her readers that, for at least four-and-twenty hours after taking it, both she and her companion retained a perfect equanimity of temper and feeling.

"That sounds something like it," suggested Helen. "perhaps Mrs. Kennett had a contract to supply cat-mint to the Government, for use by hangmen."

It was an attractive idea, just as the picture of the soft-hearted hangman who had to eat cat-mint to get satisfactorily worked up was an intriguing one. But we had to admit that it wasn't really likely.

We turned to another page.

> The blossoms of this plant (Lily of the Valley), distilled in wine, were supposed to be efficacious in curing many complaints. Parkinson says: 'The flowers of the white kind are often used with those things that help to strengthen the memorie, and to procure ease to apoplectic persons.'Camerarius setteth downe the manner of making an oyle of the flowers thereof, he says, is

very effectual to ease the paines of the gout, and such like diseases, to be used outwardly, which is this: 'Have filled a glass with the flowers and, being well stopped, set it for a moneth's space in an ante's hill, and after being drayned cleare, set it by for use.' Ettmuller recommended the flowers be dried and powdered to make a snuff good for the cure of headache; and in Germany the flowers mingled, with wine are still used for this purpose.

Well, I had seen old Jabez, who used to work with horses on our farm as far back as I could remember, bury something in a bottle in a dung-heap and leave it there for weeks, but I think it was some sort of horse-medicine, not lilies-of-the-valley.

"Perhaps Mrs. Kennett sold lilies-of-the valley to some London chemist, for making scent." said Helen.

"She might," I said, thinking as usual of all possible objections, "But lilies-of-the-valley aren't really very uncommon. She wouldn't make a fortune that way."

Miss Simpkins' other book was even less promising. Published in 1739 and entitled *The Complete Englifh Difpenfatory*, it belonged to an era when printers used the "f" like "s". We knew that "s" was intended, but the letter looked like "f", and we couldn't resist seeing how the words sounded when it was pronounced that way. We read:

Tormentillae, *Tormentil*, diftinguifhed — *Vulgaris* by *Parkinfon*, and *Sylveftris* by *Cafpar Bauhine*. It grows in Pafture Grounds and flowers in *June*. No part of this Plant is ufed in Medicine but the Root. Altho' this is moft noted for its binding Qualities, yet it is rank'd amongft the *Alexipharmics* likewife; and it is of great efteem in malignant Cafes, attended with the Flux, either of the Bowles, or the Womb; all which it is reckon'd to reftrain. *Schroder* fays there is not a better Vegetable grows than this, for all fuch Intentions. It agrees mighty well with the *White Drink*, and changes its colour to a very agreeable red; and much increafes its Efficacy in checking a Loofeness in the *Meafles*,

Small Pox or *Fevers.*

We tried repeating several times the tongue-twister in the last sentence, and agreed that we could have tried out this agreeable red drink, if only we had had "Meafles" instead of mumps. We also thought of a few "malignant Cafes" in Wilcester with which we were acquainted. On the whole, though, we thought this type of literature a bit beyond us.

I never had thought much of the idea, but Helen was disappointed, so, to satisfy her, that afternoon we made a collection of herb-like plants that grew by Elderberry Lane. Helen collected those that were in flower and pluckable (thus excluding thistles and nettles), while I made a list of the others — or, at least, of most of them. Always a lad for making notes, I made a point of carrying pencil and postcard in my pocket.

When we returned we sorted them out into six categories, namely, those which we had found on hedge-banks, in meadows, in cultivated fields and weedy corners of the same, in Aunt Sarah's derelict garden, in the woods and on the downs. From it, two points of interest emerged. But first, let me give the lists.

Hedge-banks
Agrimony, hemp agrimony, yellow archangel, avens, yellow bedstraw, white bedstraw, field bindweed, great white bindweed (which we called "lilies"), red-berried bryony, elder, red deadnettle, white deadnettle, dove's-foot cranesbill, herb robert, scabious, knapweed, flixweed, fool's parsley, cow's parsley, goat's-beard, rough hawkbit, goosegrass, horehound, mallow, meadowsweet, mugwort, black nightshade, nipplewort, ragged robin, red campion, white campion, rest harrow, dog-rose, germander speedwell, spindle, dogwood, traveller's joy, vetch, tufted vetch, tansy.
Meadows (here most of the flowers were over)
Buttercup, daisy, cowslip, dock (broad-leaved), sorrel, ragwort (abundant), dodder (on some clover-plants), black medick,

ribwort plantain, great plantain, centaury, yarrow, white clover.
Cultivated fields and field corners.

Basil thyme, yellow toadflax, ivy-leaved toadflax, red bartsia,
broom-rape (in clover-fields), sainfoin, bladder campion, corn-
cockle (then much more plentiful than today), cow-wheat, dock
(several species), gromwell, heart's-ease, hemp-nettle, corn
mint, scarlet pimpernel, knotgrass, stinking mayweed, yellow
meliot, red clover, alsike clover, charlock, poppy, shepherd's
needle, shepherd's purse, self-heal, corn sow-thistle, chickory,
creeping thistle, corn woundwort, filago, fumitory.
Aunt Sarah's Garden.

Giant bellflower, columbine, monk's-hood, goutweed, thyme,
sage, periwinkle, Star of Bethlehem, thorn-apple, henbane,
hemlock, wild lettuce, aconite, greater celandine, milk thistle,
great mullein, rose (garden varieties grown wild), guelder rose,
groundsel.
Woods

Burdock, foxglove, bugle, woodruff, enchanter's nightshade,
evening primrose, figwort, comfrey, creeping jenny, wood
germander, dark mullein, butterfly orchid, twayblade, orpine,
yellow rattle, wood sage, St John's-wort, skull-cap, wood sorrel,
wood spurge, strawberry, teazel, mercury, spear-thistle, tormentil, Solomon's seal, dog violet, wood sanicle.
Downs

Harebell, bird's-foot trefoil, carline thistle, fairy flax, burnet
saxigrage, salad burnet, eyebright, devil's-bit scabious, mouse-
ear hawkweed, juniper, hound's-tongue, kidney vetch, lady's
finger, wild mignonette, milkwort, quaking-grass, dyer's rocket,
rock rose, wild thyme.

The first point that struck us was that Aunt Sarah had certainly
been interested in herbs. There in her neglected garden were more
than we would have found in any of our own garden plots. Some of
them were "interesting" herbs, too. Monkshood, thorn-apple, henbane, hemlock, aconite, foxglove. Poisons.

The other will probably be not as apparent to the reader as it was to us. As we looked frustratedly over the wired gate into Princedun Woods, it was clear to us that that was where most of the summer flowers were. The meadows and hedge-banks had had their turn, and though the hedge-banks were still bright with blossom their flowers were all familiar and abundant species. The lowly downland flowers would be at their best a month later, and the flowers of the cultivated fields were for the most part weeds. But in the woods were orchids and foxgloves, orpine and St John's -wort, Solomon's seal, wood sanicle, dark mullein and, beyond doubt, many others in glades invisible and inaccessible. To say nothing of lilies-of-the valley. If we were to go into business as herb collectors we would have to penetrate into the woods.

"When did they stop Nadderbourne people from going into the woods?" I asked at tea-time.

"Oh, it was a long-drawn-out process," said my father. "They never said straight out, No-one to go into the wood at all. But sometimes they blocked a gate here or put a fence across there or stopped somebody walking along a little-used path."

"It began soon after the old Earl died," put in my mother. "He was a nice old chap. He used to like the villagers to come and pick flowers."

"When did he die?"

"Oh, forty years back, I suppose. Perhaps more. We were children at the time. It caused quite a stir, because he was shot."

"Shot?"

"Yes, gun went off by accident, when he was out shooting in the woods. You remember, Anne?

My mother nodded.

"Anyway, the present Earl was only an infant, and the agent and the keepers did what they liked with the estate till he grew up. The keepers never liked people in the woods. I reckon old Adam Upshot was the prime mover behind it all, turning people off the estate. He was head-keeper then. An old devil, if ever there was one."

I passed on this snippet of information, for what it was worth, to Helen.

"Well, maybe when she found she couldn't walk in the woods

whenever she liked she dug up some of the plants and planted them in her garden," she conjectured.

I allowed that might be correct but pointed out that it didn't seem to lead us anywhere. Helen, regretfully, agreed that it didn't.

"Oh, I had another talk with my Gran," she went on, brightening up, "and I asked her about that parasol that Mrs. Kennett used to carry when she went walking in the moonlight. I said it seemed a funny thing to do, but Gran said, No, it wasn't all that funny. She'd done it herself. She said that it was an old belief that the direct rays of the moon were bad for your complexion, and if you stayed out too long in the moonlight it would drive you mad."

"They were a crazy lot, in the old days," was my comment, and I meant it.

We found other things to talk about. Indeed, there was little more to be said on the subject of Aunt Sarah and the secret of Elderberry Lane. If, as we had conjectured, the clue to the secret was to be found in Aunt Sarah herself, it was remarkably well hidden. We had probed as deeply as possible into her story and had found nothing that was not straightforward and blameless. Indeed, it was so prosaic as to be boring. The only flash of interest lay in her herbs, but back in Victorian days almost every village had someone who knew about herb remedies. After all, it was necessary, with the nearest doctor six miles away in Wilcester, you couldn't send for him to cope with every childhood malady. At the most, Aunt Sarah was a modest white witch, and that was commonplace

Oh, there was one thing we noticed when we were gathering woodruff, wood sage, twayblade orchids and other flowers along the woodland edge at the far end of the lane. Glancing over the hedge into White Ox Acres, on the opposite side of the land, I saw that someone had put a fence around Golden Cap Tump. Well, not a proper fence. Just an enclosure of flimsy posts, linked by string.

I resolved to take a further look, later in the week. It suggested to me the preliminaries for an archaeologists' dig.

Chapter Five

Archaeologists were a not unfamiliar species to us in Nadderbourne. When I was at school a party of them came one summer to excavate in the Giant's Castle, the earthwork on top of Nadderbourne Down. We boys used to troop up there to "help" them in the evenings, until we outwore our welcome to such an extent that the archaeologists-in-chief persuaded Henry Upshot to patrol the approaches. We argued vigorously among ourselves about the existence of a right-of-way to the Castle, but we didn't attempt to argue with Henry and his shot-gun.

More recently, about two years before the events in this book, another party arrived to inspect the Roman road that cuts across the western corner of Nadderbourne Parish, on its precisely-ruled route from Upchester to Wilcester. They cut a couple of sections through the road, revealing its several layers. I remember there was a foundation layer of stone slabs and, near the surface, one of pebbles, which must have been brought up from the coast. When the diggers had gone, for us boys it was an invaluable mine of catapult ammunition.

The recognised programme was for the archaeologists to arrive just before harvest, though we came to understand that this had nothing to do with the, for us, climactic event of harvest but, instead, marked the end of the summer term at the universities, which generally supplied the boffins in charge. What we were now witnessing, in the Whitsun holiday week, was apparently an exploratory caper.

The savant who controlled the operation ran true to type. With beaky nose, slight chin, scrawny neck and a habit of walking with a stoop, his head thrust forward and his eyes, glinting behind their gold-rimmed spectacles, darting rapidly from side to side, he reminded me of an unhealthy White Leghorn. I learned he was Professor of Celtic, Roman and Saxon Studies at the University of Wessex and that he had written, in addition to a number of erudite papers, a book entitled *The Development of Urban Civilisation in the West of England in the Roman Era.* I borrowed a copy from the Wilcester library, partly to see what a chap like that would write but more particularly to establish lines of communication with him. Like all true Nadderbournians, I wanted to know as much as possible about what was going on in the neighbourhood, though I admit, too, that history interests me. I like to imagine what it must have been like to live inside the skins of chaps like me who stood on Nadderbourne Down to gaze over our delectable valley or who walked down Elderberry Lane long centuries ago.

White Ox Acres, in which the Tump is situated, is divided from Grove End Fields, which mark the limit of our farm, by the triangular wedge of waste and woodland known as Nimitty and by Adam's Drove. As a matter of fact, at a later date, when the demands for food production in war-time were urgent, we took over White Ox Acres and cultivated it. But at this time, 1930, we were in the very trough of the Great Depression, and White Ox Acres, like Juniper Down on the opposite side of the lane and like millions of other acres in England, lay derelict, infested by ragwort and thistles and the eldorado of multitudes of rabbits.

On my first encounter with the Professor, whose name, I learned, was Dr. Arthur Commabus, I introduced myself as a neighbour and asked a few questions about the proposed excavation — just enough to show a little knowledge but not too much.

I guessed that he would need to hire some local hands for the hard digging, though was rather disappointed to learn that he thought that six would be plenty. I knew of at least a dozen chaps who relied on casual work and for whom six weeks' work at an archaeological site would be quite a prize. However, it seemed that this was a site which did not demand a lot of heavy spade-work. He planned, said Dr. Commabus, first to investigate a series of slight earthworks, hardly visible, in the vicinity of the Tump; then a couple of minor barrows; then the

Tump itself. He was keeping the cherry till last. He thought the site would prove to be Bronze Age but was not sure. He wanted someone to give him a hand with a few preliminary trenches, so I suggested old Jimmy Jarman, who tramped off down to the Tump next morning, spade in hand.

The few weeks before haymaking are about the slackest time on a farm, I was supposed to be cultivating one of the Grove End Fields, which was lying fallow that year, but there was no urgency about the work, so I saw no harm in taking a protracted dinner-hour and walking over to White Ox Acres. On the Thursday of that week I was standing with Jimmy Jarman on the edge of a trench, at the bottom of which Dr. Commabus was stretched out, scraping at some stones with his little trowel, when a voice at my elbow exclaimed,

"Oh, what have you found?"

I half-turned, and saw a vision. I was so startled, I almost toppled over on the Professor. I don't know what Helen of Troy or Cleopatra or any of those other famous beauties of history looked like, but I would be prepared to bet that this girl had them all whacked. She was breathtaking , an idyll, a glimpse of Paradise, the fairest of all the summer flowers , Beauty personified...how was it The Song of Solomon put it? (I am great on Scripture, having spent untold hours exploring the more obscure byways of the Bible while preachers grated through interminable sermons)—"Who is she that looketh forth as the morning, fair as the moon, clear as the sun, terrible as an army with banners?"

A girl — terrible as an army with banners? Yes, indeed she was, as far as I was concerned. I couldn't have been more completely flabbergasted if old Jimmy Jarman had up with his spade and clouted me over the head with it. I had to fight hard against an overwhelming instinct to seize her and cuddle her, like I used to cuddle my teddy bear in bed at night. At the very least, I felt that the right place for my left arm was protectively around her waist, and it was all I could do to prevent it automatically moving there. It was as though I were greeting a long-lost friend with whom I had been on intimate terms. The girl wasn't a stranger; she was a part of my life that somehow had gone missing until now.

Analysing her attraction for me later I came to the conclusion that part of it lay in the contrast she supplied to most of the girls I knew. She was small, even petite, and slim, but not boyish in figure. Oh no, she had a feminine figure, right enough, — delightfully rounded in the proper places, which, of course, was what made her so cuddly. She was dark, with thick, wavy, black hair framing her oval face, and her eyes were a deep, lustrous dark brown. Unlike most of the Nadderbourne girls, whose cheeks the Nadderbourne winds and rains had painted either pink and white or golden-brown, her complexion was a delicate cream colour and her skin as soft as that of a newborn foal. Her nose was rather long, — and, when I come to think about it, all the girls I have been attracted by have had noses slightly longer than average. Her expression was normally serious, but when she smiled her lips curved up at the ends to reveal delightful dimples in either cheek.

It takes far longer to set down these details than it did for me to drink them in. They all seemed entirely familiar to me after that first glance. Or perhaps it was more than a glance, for when her exclamation first made me aware of her presence I was as dumb as a schoolboy facing a school inspector. I stared at her long enough to cause her either embarrassment or amusement, and it must have been the latter, for she smiled at me — that slow, curving smile that revealed the dimples — and said,

"Hiya. We haven't met. My name's Martita."

"Mine's Steve. Steve Maidment," I told her. "Martita, did you say?"

I'd never heard that name before.

"Sure. Don't you like it?"

"Oh, I do. I do," I hastened to assure her.

"It's only that it's...well, unusual. Martita. Do they always call you that?"

"Mom and Daddy do, and my aunties and uncles. But sometimes I get called Marty; and sometimes Teeta."

"I like Teeta," I decided.

"Well, you can call me Teeta, if you like. Now perhaps you'll tell

50

me what he's found," indicating the Professor still lying prone in the trench, entirely preoccupied and oblivious to the fact that spectators were collecting. With no information at my disposal there was little I could tell her, and I hesitated to apply the old axiom for dating, "if you don't know, make up something and let her find out whether it's true or not", lest she prove to be the Professor's daughter or something and so in a position to know more about it than I did.

But the conversation recorded above offers to the discerning reader one clue to her identity. That's right. "Mom and Daddy". Of course, I had the benefit of her accent as well, which was strange to me and very different from our homely Nadderbourne speech.

We continued talking, about the dig, and about digs in general, and about Nadderbourne and our little corner of England.

"My Dad's a farmer," I told her. "Those are some of our fields over there. That's where I'm supposed to be working,"

And I stole a guilty peep at my watch.

By thus volunteering items of information about myself, I learned through her natural desire to reciprocate, that she was American. Her name was Martita Vannecke, and her father had a potted meat factory in San Francisco. She was on holiday in England with her "Momma", who was the sister of Lady Crewkerne, and they were staying for the summer at Princedun House. She knew the Professor who had been to the House to dinner and who had, in fact, come to Wilcester at the invitation of the Earl.

Having been bred and reared in a rural society in which class distinctions were as strong as tradition could make them, I could not fail to be impressed by these aristocratic connections. I would probably have been even more so if I could have seen her Daddy's "little potted meat factory", which I later gathered, was of sufficient size and output to make him a millionaire. On the other hand, life in a village community breeds an appreciation that, social distinctions though there may be, all classes are human. We Nadderbournians were accustomed to meeting the Earl of Crewkerne and to chatting with him, man to man. Anyhow, what it amounts to is that awe at her exalted social position came nowhere near to inhibiting me in my attitude toward Martita. I chatted her up, just as I would have done with any other girl who attracted me. Not that any other girl had ever knocked me sideways at first sight like she had done. Nor was I at all conscious of the fact that, with open-necked shirt unbuttoned to the waist, shirt-sleeves rolled up, and corduroy trousers supported by a leather belt and fastened below the knees with those leather straps we called yarks, I must have seemed to her a veritable country ploughboy. We chatted away easily, and before I reluctantly went back to my work in Grove End Fields we had arranged to meet in the same place at the same time tomorrow, ostensibly to see how the excavations were progressing. And all the way back across White Ox Acres my heart kept up the chorus, "She's going to be here all the summer! She's going to be here all the summer!" I was bewitched by those lovely dark eyes, those dimples, that smile which was like the sun reappearing from behind a cloud, that vivacious little feminine figure, ... and Helen was never further from my thoughts.

I was so bemused that in the evening twilight, after shutting up the fowl-houses in the Shuffley-road fields, I walked across the intervening fields to White Ox Acres, just to gaze again at the spot where I had met my little American witch and to try to conjure up again the vision as I had first seen it.

It came as a shock to see someone still working at the Tump. My heart beat faster as I conjectured that it must be the Professor, on the track of something so important that he could not leave it till morning, in which case Martita could well be there with him. But as I drew nearer a figure with a spade extricated itself from a trench it had been digging into the Tump itself, not the outlying earthwork where the Professor had been occupied that afternoon, and stood for a minute or two, taking a breather. It was not the Professor. It was Uncle Walter.

I hurried over and confronted him.

"Uncle Walter, what in the world do you think you're up to?"

He looked at once guilty and defiant.

"It be mine. It always have been. If there be owt here, it be mine. He got no right to it, so there."

52

For him the Tump was a possible solution to the mystery of the lane. He had spent the greater part of his life searching for the treasure or thinking about where it might be hidden, and now he regarded Dr. Commabus as an interloper, who had come to steal his inheritance.

It took me a long time to persuade him to go home. I then returned to the farm and told my father and mother, who went down and talked with Uncle Walter and Aunt Maria till a late hour. When they left the cottage, they said, Aunt Maria locked the door from the inside, with every intention of sleeping with it under her pillow, so that Uncle Walter could not change his mind and escape to work on the Tump again during the night.

As expected, next morning there was trouble. The Earl and the Professor arrived in Nadderbourne, the latter furious and agitated and hell-bent on discovering the culprit. They had not far to seek, for by this time the news had spread around the village. Again my father went down to the cottage and spent an hour or two there. Confronted with the united arguments, blandishments, explanations and admonitions of the Professor, the Earl, Aunt Maria and my father, Uncle Walter eventually accepted their point of view and promised not to interfere again with the excavations.

"I think we've managed it," said my father, as they emerged, somewhat relaxed, after their arduous session, by the mollifying influence of a couple of glasses of Aunt Maria's exquisite home-made elderberry wine.

"I have my doubts," said the Professor. As we came out, Uncle Walter was still muttering to himself, "But 'tis mine, for all that."

"Perhaps it will be as well if we have a word with Police-Constable Baines," said the Earl. "He can keep a discreet eye on the site."

Which they did. So, for the next few weeks, Constable Baines was to be seen cycling along Elderberry Lane every evening just after sunset.

"Evening, Horace," Uncle Walter would greet him poker-faced, as he passed the cottage gate.

"Evening, Walter," the constable would reply, with equal solemnity.

Chapter Six

When I met Martita at the Tump that afternoon she had heard a version of the events of the previous night but wanted to know more. So, sitting there on the summit of the Tump, while we watched Jim Jarman and the Professor at work, I told her all I knew about Uncle Walter and the Secret of the Lane. I described our investigations so far, without, of course, mentioning Helen, and her eyes glowed with excitement.

"Say, that's wunnerful!", she exclaimed. "A real treasure hunt!"

"I'm not so sure that there is any treasure," I warned her.

"Aw but there must be. We can't have this poor old guy wasting his life over sumpin that doesn't exist. We'll find sumpin for him."

I soon realised I had acquired an even more enthusiastic partner in the treasure hunt than Helen. Our investigations into the Secret had lately become somewhat desultory, though very largely because we could not think of where to start looking next. The leads all seemed to have petered out. We were feeling as discouraged as a short-sighted hedgehog who, having persevered for the best part of an hour, finds he has been trying to make love to a scrubbing·brush.

With Martita I had to begin all over again. Together we examined the mystery surrounding Uncle Walter's treasure from every angle.

Was the treasure something tangible, like herbs or buried gold? If the latter, was it a treasure cache somewhere in or near the lane? Or had Aunt Sarah, by chance, heard someone, perhaps a gang of robbers, talking of it in a rendezvous down the lane? What else might Aunt Sarah have seen or heard? Something which could be used as blackmail? But surely Aunt Sarah was not the sort of person who would consider that as knowledge to be treasured? Was there any connection between the Secret and the manner of her death? That posed the question, Was there any connection between Aunt Sarah and the Upshots?

It was obvious that Uncle Walter's mind was fixed on buried treasure, and that the Golden Cap Tump was for him the most probable site. But, supposing there was treasure there, how would Aunt Sarah have special knowledge of it? Anybody could guess that there *might* be something there. Martita thought that the herbs were a good idea (I had given the credit to Miss Simpkins and had cautiously avoided any reference to Helen), but we agreed that we had taken it as far as was possible at the moment.

"Say, what about the lane itself?" asked Martita.

"Why don't we look at that? What did you say it was called?"

"Elderberry Lane."

"Does anyone know why?"

"Because of the elderberries that grow there, I suppose."

"What are elderberries?"

I explained.

"And are there a lot of elderberries growing in Elderberry Lane?"

I thought about it.

"No," I admitted. "I don't believe there are. No more than in any other place. Perhaps not so many as in some of the other lanes around Nadderbourne."

"Then why call it Elderberry Lane?"

"Perhaps there were more elder trees there when the name was given," I suggested. "After all, the name's hundreds of years old."

"Possible but not proven," said Martita. "We'll mark that one for further investigation. What's next?"

We made a mental journey along the lane, stopping to investigate each field.

"Why Spallix?"

"I don't know."

"Why Halfpenny?"

"I suppose someone used to pay a halfpenny a year rent for it."

"He had a bargain. Who was Noah?"

"An old man my father used to know."

"Who was Ensell? Who was Austin? Who was Vincent? Who was Venables? What was Glebe Land? Why call a field a Lawn? Why was the ox white?"

The questions succeeded one another inexorably, and before long I was feeling ashamed that my answer to so many of them had to be that I didn't know.

"Who was Hobbit? Was Wells the name of a man? Who was Adam? What on earth did Nimitty mean? Why did the White Ox have his acres so far from his pond? Oughtn't that field to be called Wesley, not Welsey? Why call a field a Slob? Puck sounds interesting; did he invite the fairies to come and dance on his bridge? Nadderbourne Down and Juniper Down are obvious names, but why Addle Down?"

The relentless questioning laid bare more and more areas of my ignorance.

"I guess all this will bear looking into," was Martita's opinion, and I couldn't but agree.

"Any of these persons who have fields named after them could have buried a treasure in their field," she went on. "There's Noah, and Ensell, and Vincent, and old Hobbit, to say nothing of Puck. I'll bet he knew the whereabouts of some fairy gold. Joking apart, though, I guess your old Aunt Sarah was on to sumpin, and I guess one or another of those fields holds a clue. She got wise to what one of those guys was up to."

Americans tend to be weak on or careless about chronology. One cheerful optimist from Connecticut named Maslin who once came looking for ancestors in Nadderbourne and found an entry of that name in the parish register of births for the year 1708 happily assumed that the man in question was his great-grandfather, ignoring the gap of 220 years. Martita seemed to think that Aunt Sarah would be a contemporary of the men who gave their names to the fields and would know their little secrets. But then, who was I to criticise, who had not even thought of looking for a clue in the field names? Besides, she might be right. My father had known Noah, of Noah's Close, so why should not Aunt Sarah have known one or more of the others? At any rate, the one who mattered?

"Why don't I ask my uncle about the field-names?" she put the proposition, "and you ask your folk about them, too. Then when we meet again we'll see what pieces we c'n fit together."

That sounded fine to me, more especially because it meant that we would have a perfect reason for meeting again, and probably again and again. For we were now partners in a quest, fellow investigators following a trail. I was old enough to know that there is nothing like a common interest for cementing the bonds of friendship.

Sunday intervened, with its normal boring routine of chapel services. On Sunday afternoon I walked out as usual with Helen but persuaded her that the lane to Shuffley and back across the meadows would make a pleasant change.

For some reason, I didn't feel like inspecting or discussing Elderberry Lane and its secret with Helen just then. Also we might find ourselves walking as far as White Ox Acres, and just possibly Martita might take it into her head to pay a visit to the Tump. Instinct warned me to keep these two girls apart. Monday proved a memorable day in our search for the Secret of the Lane. Martita when I met her at the Tump in the dinner hour was bubbling with excitement.

"Say, we've found it. We've got the clue to the riddle. Hi, Professor, come over here and explain to Steve."

The Professor dragged himself away from his ditch and came across, wiping his dusty hands in his trousers. From his cache of tools, documents and finds, under the shelter of a minute tent, he produced a scroll, which he unfolded and pinned to the ground by means of stones on each corner.

"It's most interesting. Most interesting," he was saying, as though holding a conversation with himself. (Which, by the way, was how he generally talked. You felt as though you were eavesdropping.) "So many of the names have endured for so long. And some have experienced some really remarkable metamorphoses."

"This map is a replica of one of the Princedun Estate in the year 1537, the year in which it passed from the Abbey of Wilcester into private hands. So we can compare the place-names with those we know today. It's quite remarkable how many of them survive, in some form or other.

But it serves, too, as a link with a more distant past. Do you know the history of your own corner of the country, young man?"

"Not as much as I would like to, sir," I replied, cautiously.

"Well, the Princedun Estate, of which Nadderbourne was a part, belonged to the Abbots of Wilcester throughout most of the centuries known as the Middle Ages," continued the Professor, getting into his pedagogic stride, "but before that it was a royal estate. It passed to the Norman kings directly from their Saxon predecessors. The earliest reference to it is in a document of King Athelstan."

I registered polite interest.

"The Professor will get there in a minute," commented Martita, encouragingly.

"Princedun in Saxon and Norman times was a quite important place. With all the appurtenances of a royal residence and with the trade that such an establishment brought, it grew almost to the stature of a small town. Princedun means "the town of the Prince". Now, what was an Anglo-Saxon prince called?"

I had a feeling that this was something I ought to know, something that had come my way at school, but it escaped me. I had again to confess ignorance.

"He was an Atheling" (and then I remembered someone called Edgar the Atheling). "An Atheling was a prince of the royal blood. And Princedun was therefore called Athelinga-dun, or Athelinga-bury. Now, you notice that I pronounce it "Adelinga-bury" rather than "Athelinga-bury", although it's spelt with a "t-h". That's because "th" in Anglo-Saxon was hard, pronounced "dh", as in "though", rather than "th", as in "thin."

So, Athelinag-dun or Athelinga-bury are exactly the same name as Prince-dun. And now here we have a lane known as Athelinga-bury Lane, and we find it's still known as Elderberry Lane. I call that a really remarkable survival. There it is, you see. Athelinga-bury Lane, leading from Nadderbourne to Princedun."

58

And he pointed to it on the old map.

"Well, I'll be dashed!" was all I could say.

Didn't I tell you, Steve, that we were on the right track? claimed Martita, excitedly. "Didn't I say there were not enough elderberries in that lane?"

"And here" resumed the Professor, "we have Addle Down, which is precisely the same name again. Athelinga-Down" — the downland belonging to the Prince."

I was still muttering to myself — Adelinga-bury"— "Adlinga-bury" — "Elderberry — Yes, it was logical. Illiterate villagers would naturally tend to transpose what had become for them a meaningless name into one which meant something. I could see how it had happened.

"There are some other interesting features,"the Professor was rambling on. "For instance, here is the little enclosure you call Ensell's Garden, and it bears the same name in 1573. So Ensell, whoever he was, must have lived before that date. Again, quite a remarkable survival.

And you see the field you call Austin's. Here on the 1537 map it is inscribed, 'To the Avonchurch monkes'. Now the Avonchurch priory was an Augustinian foundation, and that is what 'Austin's' refers to."

"So there wasn't a man named Austin, who owned the field?"

"No. Austin is an abbreviation of "Augustinian". Most interesting to find it in this connection.

Now, as we go farther along the lane we find a group of most suggestive names. They start here, you see, with White Ox Pond ...."

He indicated the spot with his finger.

"White Ox Pond. Wells Piece, Grove End, Nimitty, White Ox Acres, Welsey ... do you see their significance?" I did not. It was just as well, for the Professor had determined to explain, and a claim to prior knowledge would only have disconcerted him.

"The key to it is in these two names ... Wells Piece and Welsey ... now on this map you will see they are written "Welsh Piece" and "Welsh-ey". "Ey", of course, is an island and must refer here to a plot of dry land formerly surrounded by marshes by the little stream. The invading Saxons called the Romano-Britons whom they displaced "Welsh". When they formed their first settlements at Nadderbourne and Avonchurch, there must have been an existing British village, still inhabited, somewhere between them, and these place-names indicate where it was. We may even have a translation of its name in the term "White Ox". It may have been the White Ox Village, which in Old Welsh would be something like "Gwynych". And, of course, white oxen featured importantly in the rites of the old Celtic religion.

"Nimitty",", and he pointed to the name, "is evidently derived from 'nemet', a sacred grove, and here we have other references to a grove in "Grove End Fields" and in "Verngrove", the wood on the opposite side of the lane...

"But tell him about the most interesting bit of all, "Professor," put in Martita, "Tell him about the lane."

"The lane? Oh yes ... Athelinga-bury Lane runs, as you see, from Nadderbourne past White Ox Pond to Hobbit's Copse, and then, here, it swerves to the right and enters the forest."

"From that point, the road that leads to Avonchurch is called Avonchurch Lane, as you see. Athelinga-bury Lane winds through the forest and leads directly to Athelinga-bury, or Princedun."

"That gives you food for thought, eh, Steve?" commented Martita, after the scroll had been rolled up and stowed away and the Professor had gone back to his digging.

"So now we start all over again," I mused.

"Wherever the treasure is, it isn't in this tumulus, she pointed out. "The lane over there is Avonchurch Lane, not Elderberry Lane."

"Yes," I pondered, "Elderberry Lane ends at the gate into the woods."

"It doesn't," she contradicted. "It goes on through the woods. The gate is new, isn't it"

"Of course," I brightened up. "It's all Elderberry Lane, right up to Princedun House.

"Mm. That opens up all sorts of possibilities."

The distance between the new gate and Princedun House was

considerably greater than between Nadderbourne and the new gate. The treasure might be anywhere along its unexplored course. And what sort of treasure was it? It might be anything. Even rare herbs had to come up for consideration again.

Working in Grove End Fields that afternoon , I was struck by another thought. The next time I had an opportunity I put a question to Aunt Maria.

"Aunt Maria, just what was it Aunt Sarah said when she told you about the lane?"

Aunt Maria laughed.

"God bless the boy! Are you still harping on that?"

"Well, why not? Uncle Walter still has it on his mind".

Aunt Maria's face clouded.

"But I've had an idea, and I wanted to hear again just exactly what it was she said," I insisted.

"We-ell, I'm not sure that she didn't refer to it more than once. But the time I have in mind she said....now, let me see... what was it?.....

"If only you knew about the Secret of the Lane, what riches could be yours!"

Yes, that's it."

"Last time you told me you mentioned the word 'treasure', I reminded her.

"Oh well, 'treasure', 'riches', the same thing. What does it matter?"

"So what you are saying isn't exactly word for word what Sarah said?"

"As near as makes no difference. Why? What are you getting at?"

"Might she have said, "If only you knew about the Secret Lane", instead of "If only you knew about the Secret of the Lane"?

"I suppose she could, But that doesn't make much sense, does it?

"It might do," I said.

To be truthful, I couldn't see what sense it did make. It was just that the thought that it was the lane itself which was secret seemed suggestive. To Nadderbourne folk Elderberry Lane had no clearly defined eastern limit. At the Nadderbourne End it was indisputably

Elderberry Lane. Beyond the Coxenbourne it was Avonchurch Lane. The transition from Elderberry to Avonchurch came somewhere in between and no-one cared where. As for the track through the woods, that meant nothing to the present generation. It was indeed a secret lane, that went meandering off into the forest with no set purpose. It was never used now, except as a shooting ride on a few days in autumn and winter, and as a keeper's path.

Yet originally it has been the road from Nadderbourne to Princedun. It was the way taken for centuries by Nadderbourne folk with business at the big house. And, of course, by the owners of Princedun and their agents, keeping an eye on the tenantry of Nadderbourne. And one of the last of the Nadderbournians to tread its now grassy surface was Aunt Sarah. For that must have been where she went walking with her parasol through the woods in the moonlight. Possibly gathering herbs, as Helen had suggested.

The more I thought about it, the more certain I became that the "secret" referred to this woodland sector rather than the familiar stretches trodden daily by Uncle Walter and his cows. And then I wondered again about what, if there were no tangible treasure, Aunt Sarah might have seen. Thinking over the events, some of them wildly improbable, that might have happened in the woods, I suddenly remembered one that certainly did. The old Earl of Crewkerne had accidentally shot himself there.

I resolved to find out a little more about the accident.

Chapter Seven

The old Earl and his tragic demise were, in fact, quickly disposed of. My father knew the details.

"He went out shooting wild duck that were stubbling on Juniper Down one night in early September. The duck come down to feed on the barley-stubbles just after harvest at dusk — well, when it's nearly dark. It's usually too dark to see them when they've dropped down; you have to shoot them as they're flighting in, when you can see them silhouetted against the sky. Juniper Down used to be cultivated in those days.

Well, next morning he was found dead by a path leading back to Princedun House. He must have shot himself accidentally. Tripped over a bramble, perhaps. These things happen.

No, there was no question of suicide. The man was quite happy and cheerful when he went out. Nothing particular to worry him. Anyhow, he wasn't that sort of chap. And the coroner was satisfied it was an accident."

"What sort of man was he?"

"Very pleasant, I believe. I've always heard the old folk speak well of him. They say he was a bit under his mother's thumb. The old Dowager Lady Crewkerne was a bit of tyrant, from all accounts. He never managed to get married till he was nigh on fifty...well, forty-eight, I believe. He married Lady Emma Battesley, daughter of the Earl of Yarlington, from up in Gloucestershire. She's still alive, as you know, living in Sandford House, over by the river at Avonchurch. It's a sort of dower house for Princedun, where they put their widowed females out to grass."

"Who found the Earl after he'd had his accident?" I wondered.

"Well, I think it was old Adam Upshot, Henery's father, you know. But that wasn't until the next morning."

Just to get the facts quite clear in my mind I looked up the eighth Earl of Crewkerne in Wilcester reference library when next I went to town. All the details tallied with what my father had said. He was born in 1830, succeeded to the title in 1870, married Emma, only daughter of the fifth Earl of Yarlington, of Batchley, Gloucestershire, in 1878, had son, Montagu Evelyn Charles, born, 1879, and he died in 1880. A straightforward biography, of the sort that *Who's Who* prints by the hundred. And, as my father said, the coroner was satisfied about the manner of his death.

The results of this minor investigation were soon eclipsed by a dramatic event down in White Ox Acres. Dr. Commabus, as the climax of his excavation, drove a trench into the Golden Cap Tump and there, under a cairn of stones, discovered a veritable treasure. Although the other earthworks he had investigated in the field were apparently either Bronze or Iron Age, this was definitely Saxon. It was the burial mound of a Saxon warrior chief who had been interred with his private hoard of gold and silver.

In addition to a collection of cups, platters, vases, ornaments, weapons and other articles, all in precious metal and many of them studded with jewels, the king, as he was doubtless known, wore a golden and bejewelled belt, supporting a sword with golden and bejewelled hilt. Around his neck hung a golden and bejewelled chain, and on his head rested a golden helmet.

He was the Man with the Golden Cap. And after the Professor had got over the first excitement of disinterring one of the most important Saxon finds of the century he remembered the local legend and was excited about that, too.

"A remarkable instance of folk memory," he declared. "Most remarkable."

Mr. Josiah Pendle, our village builder, was sent for post-haste to erect a temporary building, with a galvanised iron roof, to protect the site from the weather, and two men from Avonchurch were enrolled as nightwatchmen, under the supervision of Police-Constable Baines. Like every other Nadderbournian, I went to inspect the treasure and was duly impressed by not only the obvious value of the hoard but by the beautiful workmanship of many of the objects. I felt a kind of proprietary interest in them, on account of having been present almost daily from the beginning of the excavations.

I am sure, though, that in this respect my attitude was far surpassed by that of Uncle Walter, who, having been allowed to peer into the cairn and see the treasure, predictably came away in tears, muttering, "It be mine, by rights. It be mine." He was sunk in gloom and despondency for days afterwards.

Not liking to see him so depressed, I said to Aunt Maria,

"Have you told him what we discovered about the lane?"

"Yes, I have," she said. "Anything to cheer him up. I told him that Elderberry Lane led off into the woods and that the lane along by the side of White Ox Acres was Avonchurch Lane, so that couldn't have been the treasure his mother meant. But he had an answer for that., He said, "My mother just talked about 'the Lane'. She never said what lane". It's true, you know. She didn't mention any lane by name."

That was a new and unwelcome thought to me. We had assumed that she had meant Elderberry Lane, and when we discovered that the true Elderberry Lane veered away into the woods we concluded that we needed to follow it, ignoring the continuation known as Avon Lane. But according to this evidence, it could be either. Far from restricting the scope of our enquiry, we had simply enlarged it.

I asked Aunt Maria one more question, before leaving her to comfort Uncle Walter as best she could.

"Do you think that this was the treasure that Aunt Sarah had in mind?"

"No, of course not. How could Aunt Sarah know what was in the Golden Cap Tump?"

That was my opinion, too.

The shed which Mr. Josiah Pendle had been required to erect around the Tump was necessary not only to keep out intruders and possible thieves but also to protect the dig against the weather. For the first weeks of the excavation drought had prevailed, to the extent of causing some anxiety among Nadderbourne farmers and gardeners. All the spring-sown crops and the grass-fields needed rain badly.

"Don't worry," was my father's cynical comment. "It'll rain as soon as we get the grasscutter out, to start haymaking.,"

And he was right. A May drought usually breaks in storms in early June, and this year was no exception. Now we were in June and, during all outdoor activities, we had to keep an eye on the south-western sky, for approaching rain-clouds.

With villagers almost forming a procession to visit the Tump I timed my visits with caution. Martita came down most days and obviously looked forward to seeing me. It goes without saying that I wanted nothing more than to see her. But Martita was completely innocent of the ways of village life, whereas I knew them only too well. I shrank from doing anything that would set the gossips' tongues wagging. Those tongues were as full of mischief as a colander is full of holes. Besides, I hadn't yet told Helen about Martita, or Martita about Helen. I could see trouble ahead but was all for postponing it for as long as possible.

One evening when an afternoon storm had halted our haymaking activities I walked from Grove End Fields over to the Tump and was lucky enough to find Martita there with the Professor. After inspecting what had been done during the day and engaging in desultory conversation with the Professor and watchmen, we drifted away together towards Avonchurch Lane. There was no-one about this evening, so as we strolled along the lane in the direction of Nadderbourne we slipped our arms around each other's waists, as we had got in the habit of doing when we thought we were unobserved. Teeta's head came only to the height of my shoulder, and I must say that when she rested it against my chest the curves of her body fitted in remarkably well with mine.

Nightingales were singing wholeheartedly in Verngrove, and we kept pausing to listen to them, which gave us an opportunity for an embrace and a kiss. We watched, too, a woodcock roding, flopping along erratically, on loose, owl-like wings, at tree-top level.

"A bit early in the evening for that," I commented, and then noticed that the light was beginning to fade. The nearness of the trees on our left prevented us from having a good view of the southwestern sky, but ahead we could see that slate-coloured clouds were pouring in, and thunder, which had been grumbling to itself for hours on the far side of the horizon, seemed to be nearer.

"We're in for another storm, I guess," said Teeta.

"We'd best hurry," "I decided. "Perhaps we can get as far as the ruined cottage before it breaks."

But we couldn't. Big spots of rain were splashing down as we ran past Nimitty, and the downpour started as we reached the gateway into Grove End Fields.

"Let's shelter under the straw-ricks." I called, above an ominous cannonade of thunder.

We scurried around to the lee side and huddled there, panting. But straw-ricks do not have overhanging eaves; instead, their thatched roofs tend to divert rain down their concave sides. It was going to be almost as wet there as if we were standing in the open.

I am concocting excuses. I am endeavouring to show there was really no alternative to introducing Teeta to that convenient straw tunnel, the latest occupants of which had been Helen and me.

With a decent show of hesitation I explained the position.

"Well, what are we waiting for?" demanded Teeta. "Where is it?"

I led her to the junction between the major and minor straw ricks and, bending down, revealed the camouflaged entrance.

"I'll go first, if you like. You follow."

"Right," she said. "Get a move on, Buster. I'm getting wet."

I crawled on hands and knees into the black, cosy cave in the middle of the rick. Though the tunnel itself was low and narrow, it was spacious enough in there to stretch expansively and to sit upright. Teeta tumbled in after me. I could feel her kneeling and examining her environment with her hands.

"Gee! This is swell!" she exclaimed.

I stretched out a hand and found it resting on her knee.

"Yeah," she said. "It's made for that sort of thing," and with that she threw herself into my arms.

I would not have claimed to be completely innocent in sexual matters. Helen and I had reached the stage of conducting various tentative experiments. But I soon discovered that I was a mere novice compared to Teeta. Forgotten were the facts that she was the daughter of an American millionaire and the niece of the Earl of Crewkerne and also that she was only seventeen. I was only conscious of her sweet smell, her soft skin, the warm curves of her body, her expertly groping hands. I struggled for a time to control myself.

"Say, what are you holding back for, Steve?"

"We musn't. I didn't come prepared. There's no protection."

She giggled.

"Oh, shucks to that! You don't need to worry about that. You leave that to little Teeta."

"But — but, I don't want to get you into trouble."

"Aren't you sweet! Aren't you just too considerate! But forget about it. I'm always prepared."

"Honest?"

"Honest. Now let yourself go."

So I did. And it was wonderful.

Afterwards we lay back in our dark nest, fingers entwined, exhausted. Maybe I even dropped off to sleep for a while. Presently she was tickling my stomach with a straw and I roused myself. It must be time we were moving. After several vain attempts, thwarted by Teeta, to crawl back through the tunnel, I made it to the daylight. Peeping out cautiously, I saw that the storm was almost over. A few light drops of rain were still falling on the saturated earth, but a lurid yellowish light was pervading the western sky, while a rainbow spectrum was painted on the backcloth of indigo clouds to the east.

Teeta followed me into the open air, and we brushed each other down, extracting wisps of straw from our hair and our clothes.

"Better not take that home," I grinned, taking one from the front of her blouse.

"No-one would notice, " she said, "and if they did I'd say I'd been helping with hay-making."

"That's straw, not hay."

"They wouldn't know the difference."

We kissed again, and then I walked with her part of the way through the woods, towards Princedun, before returning home.

On my way through the village street I passed the entrance to the Vicary farm and saw Helen standing at the gate. I greeted her with what I hoped was proper enthusiasm, hoping my embarrassment was well concealed.

"I haven't been seeing much of you lately, Steve," she said, regretfully.

"I know. I've been haymaking."

"Tonight?"

"Well, we were busy in Grove End Fields when that storm came on. And it came up so suddenly we had to take shelter. It was a darned nuisance. We should nearly have finished the field if it hadn't have been for that."

Then we went on to talk about the progress of haymaking in general, and the treasure of the Tump, and how Uncle Walter was taking it, and other more intimate matters.

"Would you like to come in for half-an-hour, Steve? They're all out."

For the first time in my life I refused such an offer. I knew what that could lead to, and I just couldn't have managed it again.

Chapter Eight

My mother had been sick-visiting. The convalescent was Mrs. Up-shot, an inadequate, repressed little woman who led an unenviable life in the stern company of Henry and whose lot had, by all accounts, been even more miserable when she had had her father-in-law to contend with as well. In the late winter she had been seriously ill and, although now much better, had shown no inclination to be on her feet and active again. The antagonism between Henry and so many of the villagers did not extend to his wife, who was regarded with some compassion, though accompanied by the frequently expressed opinion that "she's a poor tool. She'd do a sight better to stick up for herself."

Today, having lain in bed for so long with problems and misgivings revolving around her head, Mrs. Upshot had been unburdening herself to my mother. I came in in the middle of an account of the interview, which was being relayed to my rather bored father.

"And then she started on about Aunt Sarah. That was another thing on her mind, because of that wicked old father-in-law of hers.

"It wasn't like what they said about poor Izzie, Mrs. Maidment," she told me. "It was his fault. He kept on and on and on at the poor boy. "She's a wicked old ooman, Izzie, me boy," he'd say. "She's a witch, and in the old days she have been drownded in the pond or burned to a cinder. She bain't fit to live — aye, and if I were younger she oodn't neither.' That's what he'd say to poor Izzie, and he'd keep on at en, day atter day. "Can't think why somebody don't knock her on the haid," he'd say. "I ood, if i were young again. Twould be a hact of Christian charity, too. Evil old ooman like that ought to be put outn

70

the way. Incitin' the poor boy, that's what he were doin'. Incitin' en. And see what happened in the end."

"Why didn't you say something at the time" I asked her, and she said she would have done if Izzie had lived and had to stand trial.

"But he were daid, poor boy," she said, "and there weren't nowt to be gained by it. 'Sides, twere only my word against his. He ood have sworn he never said aught of the sort, and then twould only have made it more unpleasant at home."

"Poor woman," said my mother, "she's had a lot to put up with."

My father agreed perfunctorily. I digested the information with interest. Aunt Sarah, by all accounts, was a good woman, but it seemed that old Adam Upshot hated her bitterly, hated her enough to egg on his half-witted grandson to murder her. Why?

Later, when I could do so without the association of subject seeming too obvious, I casually asked my parents when the Upshots came to Nadderbourne.

"Oh, a bit before my time," said my father. "When the old Earl married, or so I've heard. There was a vacancy for head keeper just then, and so old Adam Upshot came over from the new Countess's home, over in Gloucestershire. To my mind, he was always hankering to get back there. Pity he hadn't gone."

My feelings as my head dropped on the pillow that night were chaotic. I thought of Teeta and relived the ecstasy of the straw cave. I thought of Helen and wondered whether I detected suspicion in her attitude. She had seemed to doubt whether hay-making accounted for all my neglect of her recently. As a farmer's daughter, she knew that the work of the farm always had to take first place, but my conscience told me I had been pushing my luck rather hard, and I wondered, uneasily, whether she had noticed it. Which, of course, shows how naive and innocent I was in those days. Anyone of more maturity would have known she would notice something amiss from the very beginning.) Then I thought of Teeta again and decided that whatever trouble resulted it was worth it. There would be a next time if I had half a chance.

To all these cogitations, Uncle Walter and his mystery took a poor third place, and, besides, I was very tired. With half-dreams of how pleasant it would be to have Teeta (or Helen either , for that matter), cuddling up to me in bed, I fell asleep.

It was not until the following afternoon, when I was side-raking hay in Orchard Close and when I had wallowed over and over again in the romantic events of yesterday, that I returned to the Secret Lane. What my parents had said had triggered off a new chain of thought.

Adam Upshot had come to Nadderbourne from Gloucestershire with or soon after the new Countess of Crewkerne. That would have been in or about 1878. His home village was a place named Blatchley. Nothing was known about his life there.

But Aunt Sarah was also a newcomer to Nadderbourne. She had come when Uncle Walter was a baby, and we had worked out that that would have been about 1867. Where had she come from? No-one knew.

So here were two strangers to Nadderbourne who were apparently enemies. Nothing had, as far as I knew, happened to cause a rift between them while they lived here. Yet, on Adam Upshot's side at any rate, the hatred was far beyond any casual antipathy. Therefore it was reasonable to suppose that the antagonism had begun elsewhere. Which posed the question, Had they known each other before they came to Nadderbourne? It seemed likely that they had.

As for the cause of the friction, I could think of any number of possible explanations. Aunt Sarah had jilted Adam. Or there had been a feud between their families.

Or she had inherited money which he thought ought to have been his. Oh, the possibilities were endless. But how to find out which of them was the true one, or whether indeed my hunch was correct, seemed an impossible task. The only promising approach to the problem would be to go to Blatchley and try to find someone who possessed information on what went on there sixty or seventy years ago. And I had no hope of doing that.

About the only thing I could do was to ask Martita to make a few discreet enquiries, if she could, about the Upshots. And I remembered to do that when I met her at the Tump in the early evening, having slipped over there before I went home from work.

Teeta was looking as ravishing as ever. Our partnership experiences of the previous evening seemed to have added a sparkle to her eye and a glow to her skin. She looked as though she wanted to fall immediately into my arms, as doubtless she would have done if there had been no spectators. But we had the company of the Professor, the two watchmen and P.C. Baines so behaved ourselves with decorum.

It was not our lucky night, for several persons came to see the excavations, so that someone was passing along the lane for most of the evening. Besides which, Alfred Honey was at work, turning hay, in Nimittty, from which, as is evident from the map, he had a good view of our straw rick. Also the horse, unhitched from the side-rake and tied to a convenient ash tree, with a pitch of new hay to keep him happy, was waiting for me. And I would have to put in an appearance at home at a reasonable time, for there were matters to be discussed about the next day's work. No, it was not our night. We had to content ourselves with a brief kiss and cuddle in the Deer Leap ditch, just inside the woods, and promised each other more delights on the following evening.

I led the horse up through Nadderbourne village. Once again my homeward way led past the Vicary farm entrance, and once again Helen was at the gate. A stony-faced Helen. One could have imagined her as Medusa, petrifying everything within range of her basilisk eye. Waves of chill disapproval engulfed me as I approached, before ever a word was spoken.

As I drew level with the gate she extended her arm and dangled a scented, cambric, embroidered handkerchief distastefully from thumb and forefinger, as though she had just retrieved it from a particularly offensive dung-heap,

"Yours, I believe," she said, icily.

"Mine?"

"Or rather, your girl friend's".

"But — but —."

"You needn't bother to deny it. Fred Bilkins found it, by the tunnel in the straw rick."

This was a block-buster that caught me completely unprepared. I stared at her for a moment, then rallied.

"Well, it must have been somebody else's...

"I said, Don't bother," she interrupted. "Fred saw you come out of the tunnel with a girl after the thunderstorm, so when he found this there, later on, he naturally thought it was mine."

Naturally. But damn and blast Fred Bilkins! Where in the hell had he been, to see us emerge from our straw cave? Still, it might have been worse. He might have given it to Mrs. Vicary.

"Go on. Take it. She'll want it again. Perhaps she only has one."

I took it, and the familiar expensive perfume floated around my nostrils, winning a momentary victory over the smell of the fidgeting horse.

"But Helen. Let me explain.."

But Helen had a sufficient innate sense of the dramatic to realise that last crack made as good an exit line as she was likely to get. She had turned her back and was stalking away, along the drive to the house. The horse started to walk on; he was eager to get home, even if I wasn't. He had taken me with him for several strides before I collected my thoughts sufficiently to stop him.

I pulled him back far enough to enable me to peep around the corner of a barn which now hid Helen from me. Now that she thought she was out of sight she had taken out a handkerchief of her own and was sobbing into it. I could see the sobs shaking her whole body. I wanted to go and comfort her. My overwhelming instinct was to rush after her and throw my arm around her and explain everything away. I cursed the horse who anchored me to the road. Then I realised that I could not explain everything away. I could not explain anything, to Helen.

I tucked the damning handkerchief in my pocket and trudged sadly home.

Chapter Nine

Nadderbourne in 1930 was a "chapel" village, largely because the rector lived at Shuffley, over the hill, with which village we were "twinned" to form one parish, Shuffley received high priority in the matter of this good though aged man's time, and Nadderbourne was left very much to work out its own salvation. Which it did at the Primitive chapel.

We were strong Sabbatarians, refusing to do any but necessary work on Sundays., Public opinion was heavily in favour of this taboo and also of attendance at Sunday services. Going to chapel on Sundays was *the* thing to do. Rebels who flouted the convention were made aware of widespread displeasure. Even those who were not enthusiastic evangelicals, like quiet, sedate Aunt Sarah, were almost always at the Sunday evening service. Many of us adolescents attended, too, because there was little else to do on Sunday evenings, especially in winter. And at least the services were lively. Anyone who could play a musical instrument took it along, so there were always three or four cornets, several violins, a drum, a euphonium, and ophicleide (which its owner called a "serpent"), a cello, a couple of harmonicas, a bass horn and one or two others. The hymns we sang mostly had choruses, so our services were noisy, if nothing else. Some of the congregation were good part-singers; some simply shouted at the tops of their voices. In summer the unofficial band would sometimes meet half-an-hour before service time at the corner or outside the village shop and play tunes before marching in procession to the chapel. It added a little colour to village life.

The chapel was under the pastoral care of a minister resident in

Wilcester, who generally managed to make the six-mile journey, in pony-and-trap, about once a quarter. For the other Sundays it relied on local preachers, — laymen who arrived in trap, on horse-back, on bicycle or on foot. The preacher would arrive in time for the morning service, be entertained for lunch by one of the chapel members and stay for the evening service. Sometimes he could also be persuaded to give a talk to the afternoon Sunday School. The Maidments took their turn at entertaining the preacher.

Apart from the Sunday services, the chapel was a focal point of village life. There were special services, with lengthy preparations to be made for them, on Good Friday, Whitsuntide, Harvest Festival and Christmas. Tea meetings, which gave the womenfolk a chance to show their abilities and to meet for a good gossip, were always features of these festivals. Throughout autumn and winter there was a programme of week night meetings, ranging from Band of Hope (at which we youngsters were taught the principles of total abstinence from intoxicating liquor) to Services of Song (a kind of sacred concert performed by a visiting choir). Both the Sunday School and the Band of Hope had a Christmas treat, with tea, Christmas tree, presents and an entertainment (a conjuror or a Magic Lantern if obtainable). And a red letter day of the summer was the Sunday School Outing, usually to the farm of a public-spirited "chapel" farmer within six or eight miles, where we had pony rides, romped in hay-fields, sledged down steep hills and enjoyed strawberry teas.

With all this activity, one would think that the religious life of Nadderbourne was pretty adequately catered for. But no. More was necessary. There were sinners outside the fold. There were backsliders. There were young people who had never committed themselves to joining the children of God. These had to be prevailed upon. The straying sheep had to be rounded up and brought into the fold. So, from time to time, the chapel organised an evangelistic crusade.

One such crusade took place in 1930. Usually it would have been planned for the autumn, when harvest was over, the evenings were drawing in, and time could be spared for such matters. But, for some reason, this one was to occupy two weeks between haymaking and harvest. It therefore intrudes right into the middle of our story and, as it happens, made a considerable impact on it.

The visiting evangelist was a massive, deep-voiced probationer minister, the Reverend Ephraim Rackett. Mr. Vickary fetched him from Wilcester station in his pony and cart and took him to Mr. Josiah Pendle's, where he was to stay. Those of us who saw him arrive felt rather sorry for this large, perspiring man, clad in black raiment in the middle of the heat-wave that was following the thunderstorms of hay-making. We need not have been concerned. When he got going in the pulpit on Sunday evening he stripped off, progressively, coat, waist-coat, collar and tie and rolled up his shirt sleeves. He was also an excellent violinist, performing with the verve and zest of a concert virtuoso, his long hair tumbling over his sweating face. We found him intriguing.

On afternoons he would either sit under the big apple tree on Mr. Pendle's lawn or would take long walks through the fields, communing with himself and preparing his verbal assault on the ungodly for the evening ahead. On one such walk down Elderberry Lane he met, as was inevitable, Uncle Walter.

On this afternoon he had, as was his frequent practice, his violin with him. He was sitting on a gate leading into Nimitty, playing cheerfully to himself, when Uncle Walter appeared, sauntering along with his cows. Uncle Walter was a bit of a musician himself. His instrument was the bass viol, which he used to play in the chapel "band", until he drifted out of the habit. For Uncle Walter was by way of being a backslider.

For the evangelist he was, of course, a sitting target. A man who habitually took two hours or more to manoeuvre his cows between his meadows on the edge of Juniper Down back to the village could hardly put on speed to escape an importunate stranger.

The evangelist was tactful. He was an efficient fisher of men. He first used his violin as a bait. Uncle Walter stopped to listen to him.

"I see you appreciate music," said the evangelist, after a bit.

Uncle Walter acknowledged that he did.

"I used to play," he admitted. "The bass viol."

"Not much of an instrument to play on its own," commented Mr. Rackett. "You need an orchestra or band."

Uncle Walter confessed that he used to perform at the chapel but had not done so lately. With a lead like that, the evangelist could hardly fail, but he played his quarry astutely. He got Uncle Walter to talk about himself - a topic which few can resist. Uncle Walter told him about his cows, about his routine, about his past, about his ambitions (such as they were) and so, eventually, about the Secret of the Lane.

Then the evangelist struck. From his pocket he extracted a small black New Testament and, with practised adroitness, opened it immediately at the thirteenth chapter of the Gospel of St Matthew and read:

> The kingdom of heaven is like unto treasure hid in a field; the which when a man hath found, he hideth, and for joy thereof goeth and selleth all that he hath, and buyeth that field.

"There is your treasure, Walter Kennett," declared the preacher.

The analogy touched Uncle Walter on a vulnerable spot, for over the past years he had often considered the idea of buying White Ox Acres but, with his usual procrastination, had put off action. Now that a treasure had indeed been found there, he had been bitterly reproaching himself. As the preacher continued his assault, Uncle Walter turned over this new concept of life in his mind, and suddenly the light dawned. Many times afterwards, at the chapel. I have heard him describe his emotions:

> "I saw the treasure I had searched for so long as a mere jack-o'-lantern, leading me into the mire. And I turned right about, and saw the real treasure, and I claimed it as mine. I knelt there in the dust and gravel, and Elderberry Lane was the road to Paradise. The new-mown hayfields shone with light, like the green sky in the west after sunset at midsummer. The starlings grub-hunting in the fields were chattering about the glory of God. The poppies were red as my sins which were washed away;

the clover-heads by the roadside were white as my new-cleansed soul. I had never seen the sky so blue; never smelt the honey-suckle so sweet; never before heard the bees humming the bass viol's part to the angels' song as they gathered their honey. I knelt and praised the Lord, and the sheep grazing in White Ox Acres answered Amen. The sun came from behind a white cloud and poured its light on me, and I shouted for joy, and all the rustling cornfields took up the cry. It was Glory Day for me! Praise the Lord!"

I often felt that there was a poet going to waste in Uncle Walter. Once he settled down again, though, to his usual pedestrian life, the inspiration faded a bit. His "testimony" became stereotyped, with few alterations to the above, as though he had learned his set piece by heart.

Still, I thought I had some inkling of how he felt at that moment. Had I not shared similar emotions, though perhaps of not quite the same intensity, when I first saw Martita, and on that evening in the straw cave, and especially on another occasion yet to be related? It occurred to me that perhaps religious and sexual ecstasy are not so very far apart.

With the evangelist still in full cry at his revival meetings, the news of Uncle Walter's conversion spread quickly around Nadderbourne and to the neighbouring villages. Uncle Walter, whose pew in the chapel had seldom been occupied by anyone but Aunt Maria for some years past, now attended every meeting, and many crowded in to hear him describe his spiritual experience, as he was called upon to do nightly. My parents, loyal but undemonstrative chapel members, were gratified but rather embarrassed by it all. So was Aunt Maria, who nevertheless accompanied Uncle Walter and supported him, though, I think, privately of the opinion that he was making a fool of himself. The efforts of our Nadderbourne chapel folk to compromise between, on the one hand, the enthusiasm they felt it their duty to be continually stirring up and, on the other, their innate regard for respectability and convention were sometimes intriguing to watch.

But if my parents and Aunt Maria and the other more sedate chapel members were a little uncomfortable about Uncle Walter's behaviour, that was nothing compared to what was to follow. As for me, my ego was about to go through an experience comparable to that of an apple in Uncle Walter's cider-press. My soul was on the verge of being put through the mangle.

As the mission proceeded, few who lived within hearsay and rumour range of Nadderbourne escaped hearing about it, and so I ought not to have been surprised when Martita started to question me. But I was. The social and cultural gap between us villagers and the family up at the House was so wide that I could not conceive that the latter would ever hear about the goings-on at the chapel, let alone be interested in them. In spite of the intimacy that had developed between us, all the barriers were not yet down, and I felt much as I would have done if she had walked into the bathroom just as I was getting into the bath.

"What are these camp meetings I hear you are holding down in Nadderbourne?"

"Camp Meetings?"

"You know what I mean. The tent meetings. The mission, or whatever it is you call them."

Rather reluctantly, I gave her a brief accounts of Rev. Ephraim Rackett's campaign.

"What happens?"

"At the meetings? Oh, they have hymns and prayers and Bible readings, like in an ordinary service. Then the evangelist gets up and gives a stirring address, calling on everyone to repent of his sins and be converted. And sometimes somebody gets overcome and goes out to the front, and the evangelist prays with him...."

"And all the people shout 'Amen' and 'Glory' and 'Praise the Lord!' — and then somebody starts singin' a chorus like "Hallelujah to the Laimb, who died on Mount Calvary!" — and everybody joining in...."

"Hey, you seem to know all about it!"

"Sure. I bin to lots of meetin's like that. My Grandmaw likes to bundle me off to some downtown mission hall, Sundays. Mom'n Daddy, they don't think much of it, but Grandmaw was brought up on camp meetin's, down in Louisiana, and she loves 'em. So do I . I like to hear the old characters get wound up and carried away. Say, I'm gonna come along with you, Sunday."

I was aghast. It was as though, having come into the bathroom as I was about to start my ablutions, she had announced that she was going to stay to watch the performance.

"Teeta! You can't"

"And who says I cant?"

"But, Teeta, you don't know anybody. And they don't know you. And it'll be all strange. And...."

I might as well have saved my breath. I might have known that once Martita had made up her mind about anything it would need more powers of persuasion than I had to alter it. I even swore I would stay away that evening or, if I came, I wouldn't sit with her — which, of course, had no effect at all, for all she said was,

"And who's asking you? I can sit with myself, thank you. I've got two legs to get there, and a bum to park on."

With a leaden heart and a sick feeling in my stomach I arranged to meet her near the keeper's cottage on Sunday evening and escort her to chapel.

"Make it early enough. I want to hear the band play in the open air and then march with them to the Lord's house. *And* I want a front seat!"

No slipping in late and occupying the back seat, as I had half-hoped. I wasn't to be spared a single thing.

With this appalling prospect before me, I felt there was nothing to be gained by trying to keep it from my parents. I told my mother. Though normally equal to any emergency, she was hit speechless for a moment; then, rallying, she began to ask questions about Martita. How long had this been going on? How well did I know her? What sort of a girl was she? What relation was she to the Earl? Who was her father? How long was she staying at the House? Basic things like that. "Well," she said. "I hope she'll like what she sees and hears."

Next day she returned to the subject.

"Your father says that if your new girl is coming to chapel on Sunday night, she'd better come to tea as well."

That was a possibility that hadn't occurred to me. At first I found it as alarming as the forthcoming attendance at chapel, and I instinctively began to make excuses, but my mother would have none of them. Once she had made up her mind, she was as determined as Martita. I should of course, have realised that this is an ubiquitous feminine trait.

And, needless to say, when I broached the matter with Martita, hoping, though with little real optimism, that she might decline, she accepted with alacrity.

"Say, that's real nice of your folks. Sure I'll come."

So there I was, completely committed, and wishing to God I could sicken for mumps again.

When we met at White Ox pond on Sunday afternoon Martita was wearing a short pink dress, which contrasted well with her black hair, silk stockings, and one of those hats, then fashionable, which now remind us of an inverted coal-scuttle. She also wore black silk gloves and a demure expression. She looked so smashing that I wanted to kiss her there and then, but she stopped me, saying I would spoil her make-up. I couldn't see that she was wearing any, but she said she was, so I guess she was pretty skilful in its application.

Uncle Walter, mindful nowadays of the necessity of being on time for evening service, had taken to hurrying the cows along a little (doubtless to their bewilderment) and was already in the cowshed, milking. Aunt Maria, however, was in the garden, and we waved to her. Then came the ordeal of walking up the village street. We passed only old Jimmy Jarman, out with his dog, but were uneasily conscious (or, at least, I was) of eyes watching from behind curtains. I felt particularly uncomfortable when passing the Vicary farm, though no-one was in sight. I could seem to see Mrs. Vicary pursing her lips and slamming down her book with a thump, and Helen, after one stony stare, fleeing upstairs to commune with her pillow. Naturally, for this stage of our walk Martita chose to slip her hand through my arm, and, as she seemed to do it quite subconsciously, I couldn't very well draw my arm away.

At home I introduced her to my mother and my little sister Mary Ann, who was nine but only about six inches shorter than Martita. My mother invited us to go and sit in "the front room", but instead we went out to walk in the garden and the orchard, and I showed her my rabbits, and the horses having their weekly rest in the meadow, and the calves — at least, those that could be approached without having to paddle through the muddy, dung-strewn yard. We had no milking cows, but my father was in the meal-shed, preparing the afternoon feed for the pigs, who were yelling with impatience, so I steered her clear of there, until he was fit to be seen. Martita appeared to be entranced by it all.

Everyone assembled promptly for tea, for once, even Tom and Stan, my two brothers, turning up well scrubbed and bashful without my mother having to delay proceedings while she sent out scouts to see if they were anywhere in the vicinity, as usually happened. My father said grace, and we were off to a stiff and shy start.

However, Martita proved adept at putting everyone at ease, and my father and mother soon warmed to her. She enjoyed her food, which commended her to my mother, and was not afraid to ask for a second helping of cream. She particularly liked my mother's "Melting Moments" — small cakes which seemed to melt in one's mouth, in the making of which my mother excelled — and asked her for the recipe. When my father tentatively asked a few questions about farming in California she gave some surprisingly informative answers. It appeared that, to provide part of the supplies for his potted meat factory, her father had a ranch and a beef feed lot up in the northern part of the state, towards Oregon, and Martita chatted knowledgeably of Herefords and Aberdeen-Angus, of the range problems imposed by bears and coyotes, and of fattening rations and daily weight-gains. As we had never before got around to those subjects, I was surprised and impressed. So was my father, and the two boys stared as they would have done if I had brought home a kangaroo.

After tea, Martita tried to insist on helping with the washing-up, but my mother was adamant,

"No," she said, "Steve will give me a hand with that."

This was news to me, washing-up being a chore I generally managed to escape, but, challenged like this, I could hardly make excuses, so I settled down with a good grace and the tea-towel, while Mary Ann took Martita by the hand and led her away. Mary Ann had often said she wished she had a sister, and it was obvious that Martita would, in her opinion, fill the role ideally.

So far, so good. Neither Martita nor my family put a foot wrong. Now for the main hurdle.

I managed to delay setting out for chapel for five or ten minutes, thus giving time for the band to get well started at the open-air meeting. A small crowd had already collected, and were singing lustily, so we were able to join it without attracting too much attention. After a few hymns, Mr. Rackett prayed and then exhorted everyone to follow the band to the chapel. We did so in good marching-time, to the strains of "Hold the fort".

Our family pew was five rows from the front, just behind that of Mr. and Mrs. Joseph Nutbeam. The two boys went in first, then my mother, then Mary Ann (who insisted on sitting next to Martita), then Martita and myself, and finally my father. The Vicarys sat one row back, on the opposite side of the aisle. People came flocking in, till the chapel was packed. Chairs had to be fetched from the schoolroom and placed in the aisle for the latecomers. I felt myself trapped.

Mr. Pendle, the builder, who was also chapel steward, shuffled around, opening the windows as wide as possible, but it was mid-July and already the place was becoming permeated with the aroma of sweating bodies. Singing, especially at the volume we reached, made us even hotter. The Rev. Ephraim Rackett, after his custom, began to strip off his outer garments, and many of the men in the congregations began to follow his example, removing their jackets and laying them decorously across their laps. I would have liked to do the same but hadn't the nerve, with Martita sitting by my side. I glanced at her and wished I felt as cool as she looked, in her short-sleeved, short-skirted, low-necked dress. She was even wearing one glove still.

The meeting proceeded along the expected lines. It was the conventional "hymn sandwich", each prayer, Bible reading and other item being sandwiched between hymns. The Rev. Ephraim Rackett, having by now dispensed with all except his trousers and shirt and having rolled up his shirt sleeves and unfastened two of his front shirt-buttons, launched into an eloquent and impassioned address. Exclamations of "Amen", "Praise the Lord!", "Hallelujah!" and similar ejaculations were forced from the more emotional members of the congregation, but when the sermon ended with the usual appeal for converts no-one staggered up to the front. Perhaps the obstacle of the chairs in the aisle deterred them.

We sang another hymn, "Come to the Saviour, make no delay", during which some, though not many, of the congregation, left. Then we launched into the more intimate part of the proceedings, the "after-meeting". This was where members of the congregation took part, with prayers, testimonies, choice of hymns and so on. Its emotionalism always made me feel so embarrassed that I generally slipped out, and tonight I would have given anything to be able to do so, but everyone else in our pew and those around stayed put, so I had to do likewise.

"Would any brother pray with us?" invited the evangelist.

Mr. Pendle predictably obliged. Then Mr. Nutbeam followed, and the interjections became more numerous. Things were warming up. "Amen", said my father. "Amen" said a clear little voice on the other side of me. I glanced at her in surprise, but she was bending down with her eyes closed.

Mrs. Charlesworth, who often took the lead in this fashion, started up a hymn, in her piercing voice, "Someone will enter the pearly gates, Shall you? Shall I?" The congregation, like a trained choir, let her sing the main part and chimed in at the appropriate points with "Shall you? Shall I?" and then a second muted "Shall you? Shall I?", like an echo. Even in my uncomfortable, tense, perspiring state I could not help noting that it was quite effective.

"Would Mr. Kennett like to give his testimony?" called the preacher, and Uncle Walter slowly stood up.

"For all my life." he declared, with some exaggeration, for his mother hadn't mentioned the Secret of the Lane till he was a grown man and married,. "for all my life I've been searching in Elderberry Lane for a treasure, which my mother said was hidden there. And now, praise the Lord, I've found it....."

He went on to describe his meeting with the evangelist and how the light of heaven broke on him.

"I knelt there in the dust and gravel, and Elderberry Lane was the road to Paradise."..."Praise the Lord!"..."the new-mown hayfield shone with light "..."Bless His Name!"..."The poppies were red as my sins which were washed away" ..."Hallelujah"..."I knelt and praised the Lord" ..."Glory"..."And the sheep grazing in White Ox Acres answered Amen!", from all quarters of the building..."It was Glory Day for me!"... "Praise the Lord"...there now, old Mr. Pendle had said it for him, and Uncle Walter's testimony was at an end. But before anyone else could utter a word, someone else struck up a chorus.....

"I'm living on the mountain, underneath a cloudless sky...."

It was a clear, youthful, female voice on my immediate right. It was Martita! I was stunned, The chapel swam and swayed as though shaken by an earthquake. I wished it would collapse completely and swallow me up.

She knelt with her head propped up by her two hands, one of them still black-gloved, and her elbows on the shelf provided for hymn-books. Her eyes were fixed on a point on the front wall, about in the middle of the painted text which proclaimed "Enter Into His Courts With Praise", and she sang with girlish sincerity.

"I'm livin' — on the mountain — underneath a cloudless sky"

"Praise God," said someone.

"I'm drinkin' — at the fountain — that never shall run dry;
Oh yes, I'm feastin' — from the manna — from a bountiful supply,
For I am dwellin' in Beulah Land."

It was an old hymn, not very familiar to me, though I think I had

heard it once or twice before, but the older folk knew it. Old Mr.
Pendle would even repeat the verses, or some of them, and as Martita
finished the chorus he launched into one.

> Far away the noise of strife upon my ear is falling,
> Then I know the sins of earth beset on every hand;
> Doubt and fear and earthly joys in vain to me are calling;
> None of these shall move me, from Beulah Land.

As with Martita, his effort was almost a solo, but this time when
the chorus was reached they were ready. The tune has a good martial
drum-beat, and the congregation went into it like an army on the
march. Martita was still singing, but her voice was hardly audible in
the general torrent of noise. When she had first struck up, my father
had directed a perplexed gaze at her, and my mother, after a hurried
glance, had closed her eyes and I could see her lips moving in prayer.
But now they were singing, too.

When we came to the end of the chorus the second time, and the
uproar was beginning to die down a little, what should Martita do but
to start on it for a third time..

"I'm livin'" – on the mountain – unnerneath a cloudless sky....
pom–pom..."

"Amen!" called Mr. Nutbeam, just in front of me.

The congregation were all in favour of it and chimed in with
enthusiasm. All except the Vicarys, in the pew opposite. As Martita
reached the bit about the cloudless sky, Helen could stand no more.
She jumped up and made hurriedly for the door, her handkerchief to
her mouth as though she urgently needed to be sick. After a pause of
a few moments, her family followed her. Their exit was rather
undignified, with much scraping of chair legs as they pushed passed
the overflow seated in the aisle. I could tell that from the sound effects,
though I dared not look. I kept my head buried in my arms, with
Martita carolling away happily in one ear and my father adding a bit
of bass in the other.

In the depths of my mortification I thought with compassion of

Helen. One part of me longed to go out and comfort her, as I would have done a few months earlier, but I knew that any understanding between Helen and myself was now irretrievably smashed. She would never forgive me for this. And what had I got in exchange? This bewitching siren who was still gazing, with an angelic expression, at the wall above the preacher's head, as though she were seeing visions. What was she? A saint? I did not know whether I had the character and stamina to sustain life with a saint. Yet what an adorable, cuddly creature she was! As though sensing my thoughts, she dropped her left hand on to the seat between us and, still singing, sought mine and gave it a squeeze. Like the hymn said, I was in Beulah Land.

The service was over and we had extricated ourselves from the obstacle course of scattered chairs in the chapel aisle. The preacher and several of the chapel leaders had shaken our hands at the door, reserving a specially warm handshake and a word of appreciation for Martita, I noticed. The family parties stood, for a moment, poised to go their separate ways, while exchanging mundane greetings.

My mother looked doubtfully at Martita.

"Would you like to come back for a cool drink before you go home?" she asked.

"Oh, no thanks, Mrs. Maidment. Gee, I'd love to but my folks will be expectin' me home. Say, wasn't that wunnerful!"

My mother seemed uncertain as to how to reply to that.

"It was, certainly an experience", she agreed, cautiously.

"Aw, I think it was great. I haven't enjoyed a camp meetin' so much since my Grandmaw took me to one run by the Congregation of the Cherubim somewhere downtown in San Francisco. My Grandmaw would have loved this tonight ....just loved it. Thank you for lettin' me come."

"And it sounded to me as though somebody else was enjoying it," I remarked, when goodnights had been said and we were on our way Princedun-wards.

"Sure I did. Didn't you?"

"No," she went on. "I don't think you did. You're so straight–laced 'n sober, Steve, sometimes I think you've bin dipped in concrete some time. You wanna learn to let yourself go."

She slipped her hand happily and cheerfully through my arm, gave me a squeeze and then led me, in a proprietary manner, down the street, oblivious to the eyes of a group of worshippers still in a knot outside the chapel behind us. We were passing the gate of the Vicary establishment again, too.

Proceedings at the chapel had been long-drawn-out, and the long summer evening was fading. Since Teeta had been paying frequent visits to Nadderbourne she had acquired a key to the padlock fastening the gate that barred the Princedun section of Old Elderberry Lane, and she now extracted it from her hand–bag. Once we had passed through and were under the canopy of forest trees the light was several degrees fainter. We felt a little like Babes-in-the-Wood and walked with our arms around each other's waists, for reassurance.

After the noise and heat of the revival meeting, the forest was delightfully cool and silent. I drank in its peace in great gulps and began to recover my equanimity.

On a hot sunny afternoon in July flies, midges and other stinging and biting insects make the woods a purgatory, but in the cool of the evening these disappear, their place is taken by multitudes of moths, particularly the white Ghost Swift moths that drift about like weightless wraiths, by blundering cockchafers and by glow-worms. We found a colony of these last, flaunting their green lamps on a bank where wild strawberries were ripening above a carpet of wild thyme, and we stayed examining them for a time, picking one or two and letting them illuminate our hands with their cool, clear light. Lime trees had at some time been planted on either side of Elderberry Lane, and the air was redolent with their sweet scent, and that of the honeysuckle twining around hazel thickets.

The season for nightingale's song was past, and no other bird voices enlivened the dusky glades. Occasionally rustling amid the leaves and bushes indicated the passage of some animal – perhaps a deer, perhaps a rabbit, perhaps only a hedgehog, which makes a rumpus out of all proportion to its size – but we saw none.

About halfway to Princedun House we came to a clearing where woodmen had been at work, cutting hazel for sheep-cribs back in the winter. Such a clearing gives, for a few years, the lowly woodland flowers, such as primroses, violets and wood anemones, a chance to bloom in profusion without being smothered by the taller, coarser growth that later intrudes. Birds, too, appreciate the sense of space and the clear view all around them while they are seeking for food. The dense forest is a place of great danger, where predatory creatures find ample cover for sudden assaults and ambushes.

This glade was surrounded by oaks on all sides but one, which was marked by an irregular row of tall wellingtonias. As we entered it we were conscious of an insistent, metallic whirring, as though three or four alarm clocks had been set off.

"Nightjars," I told Teeta. "There's one over there by that big fir."

I pointed to the nearest wellingtonia, which was evidently providing a perch for a male nightjar, intent on presenting his tireless challenge to his neighbours.

"Nightjars?" queried Teeta.

"A night bird," I amplified. "Perhaps you call them night-hawks or goatsuckers in America? They're about the same size as a cuckoo, with long wings. That ticking noise is what they think is a song."

We stood still for a moment, and suddenly the avian mechanism ceased its clatter. For a few seconds nothing happened, and then we saw the apparition.

It was a spherical dark ball with a rather fuzzy outline, about the size of a football and equipped with two bright white eyes. It came on a zigzagging course across the clearing but unmistakably moving in our direction. And as it approached we heard several loud, explosive notes, like pistol-shots.

Fortunately, I knew what this was. I had watched similar displays before. It was the courtship ritual of the male nightjar, which when displaying, beats its wings in a full circle, so that they meet both above and below the body. This is done in flight so rapidly that one gets the impression of a sphere with blurred edges. On the secondary feathers of the wing are two white marks which are in the right positions on the sphere to appear as eyes. And, as it flies, at frequent intervals the bird beats its wings with extra vigour, bringing them together over its back with a loud crack, like a firework.

The explanation is therefore quite prosaic. Many other birds and animals behave extravagantly when courting. That is what I tell myself now, sitting in a familiar well-lit room, with the dog curled up at my feet. It felt far otherwise in the dark and lonely woods. In spite of knowing what was happening. I felt the hairs on the back of my neck rising like a dog's bristles. The dark sphere that was the nightjar continued to come at us on a crazy, zig-zag course. It looks like a disembodied head, with those staring white eyes, bobbing about over the ferns.

As it approached to within a few yards, before swerving away into the trees, I had to keep a firm grip on my self–control. Panic was near. As for Teeta, she threw her arms around my waist and buried her head in my chest, shuddering. She uttered a little moan of fear. If she thought she was seeing a ghost I couldn't blame her. Displaying nightjars must be responsible for many a story about woodland spooks and bogeys.

When the nightjar had satisfied his curiosity and had retreated to an oak tree behind us, where he had cheerfully resumed his clock–like song, Teeta half–released me and looked into my face.

"What was it?" she whispered.

I explained.

We stood, close together, listening to the nightjar solo. Then an owl glided across the clearing, on noiseless wings, as ethereal as a wisp of thistledown.

The white ghost swift moths drifted, like globules of gossamer, around our legs.

"This wood is enchanted," breathed Teeta. "It belongs to a fairy–tale book. Come over here."

Finding my hand, she led me to the edge of the glade, where a fern forest, margined by foxgloves, flourished.

"It's as good a place as we shall find," she said, sinking down into a nest of fern and drawing me with her. As the crushed ferns shaped themselves around our bodies, our lips met and our arms clutched each other like children gripping a new toy which someone is trying to take away from them.

Until that moment I had been a prey to doubts. The straw cave, the Deer Leap and our other private encounters had receded into the background to make room for this new image of a pious, religious–minded Martita who seemed little short of an embryo saint. I couldn't reconcile the two. How could I expect this wonderful girl, whom only an hour or so ago I had seen gazing, with the face of an ecstatic angel, at the text above the Rev Ephraim Rackett's head, as though she was seeing a vision, – how could I expect her to tumble with me in the bracken? Now that this was what was happening, I still felt inner misgivings. It was as though my mother had sent her best porcelain tea-set out to the harvest fields for the farm men to drink cider from.

However, the proximity of Teeta's delicious little body did not help introspective analysis. I was just entering into the spirit of the hour and forgetting all the incongruities that had been worrying me when she drew away and knelt on the crushed fern, surveying me.

"Gee, isn't this wunnerful, Steve," she breathed. "It's magic. Let's make love."

With that she stood up, stretched out her arms to the fading golden light of the western sky, then, turning, started fumbling with her clothes.

"It unbuttons down the back," she said, indicating the pink dress. "I can't reach very well. Do it for me."

Too surprised and excited to utter a word, I stood up and, with inexpert fingers, started to do as she bid. All the time she was fiddling with those buttons she was doing the same with mine, and, as I finished, my trousers fell down around my ankles. With a swift movement, she drew her frock over her head and tossed it on to the ferns. Stooping, she started to unfasten her suspenders and remove her silk stockings. My instinctive reaction was to grab for my trousers and pull them up to the their proper level; then I realised how unreasonable that would be and so stood, waiting for her to make the first move.

Stockings divested, she posed before me, a slim slip of a girl, though with all the proper curves, clad in only a white vest and a pair of brief, blue, frilly panties. She moved towards me and we embraced. I kissed her and kissed her again and again, and she responded by holding me tighter. Then I was conscious of her hands, behind my back, starting to manipulate my vest and underpants. Her delicate fingers pushed the one up to the small of my back and the other down over my thighs.

I wriggled with uncontrollable embarrassment.

"You can do the same for me," she whispered.

I did.

We broke apart, and I stepped out of my clothes, whipping my vest over my head. She did the same, and we stood, admiring each other in the soft, luminous twilight.

Apart from my little sister on bath-nights, I had never before seen a completely naked female form. It was a shattering experience. This was far different from furtive fumblings in the jet blackness of the straw cave. My eyes took in every detail of her exquisite figure, from the glossy black hair tumbling about her pale, oval face to her dainty toes flexing on the dark-green fern.My whole body throbbed and tingled with excitement and anticipation.

Her shining dark eyes looked into mine.

"You're wunnerful, Steve," she whispered, and she threw herself forward into my arms.

No-one who has never made love on a summer night in a honeysuckle-scented English wood can imagine the wonder and ecstasy that were ours. At the beginning I hung back, pestered by misgivings and feelings of guilt.

"Don't be so worried, Steve," said Teeta, sensing my half-hearted approach. "Let yourself go."

So I shook off my inhibitions and surrendered to the joy of the moment. Simultaneously we reached a peak that sent rainbow flashes searing our brains and left us semi-conscious and gasping. Then we lay quietly, till snuggled close together, listening to the continuing chatter of the love-inspired nightjars and appreciating the coolness of a little wayward breeze that from time to time caressed our heated bodies.

Presently, perhaps half-an-hour later, Teeta sat up and announced that we ought to be going. Then she fell on me for one final embrace. "Thank you, thank you, dear Steve. That was heavenly."

I was startled. It had been such a wonderful experience for me that it didn't seem right that I should be thanked for it. That a girl would say, Thank you, was something that had never occurred to me.

At last we were dressed again. It was now nearly dark and, although experience had shown me that Teeta's people were remarkably tolerant about the hours she kept, I realised that she ought soon to be home. So we left the nightjar glade and walked, arms still around each other, till we came to the demarcation line between the forest and the lawns that surrounded the imposing mock-Gothic mass of Princedun House. There, with a final goodnight kiss, we parted, Teeta to run lightly across the close-clipped grass to the towering porch, I to retrace my steps along the woodland path to Nadderbourne.

And as I walked I trembled, not only from physical exertion but from a reliving of the soul-shaking events that had racked me that evening. Dominant above all was the riddle presented by my dainty Martita. How could a girl, how could anyone, display such devotion as she had shown in the chapel and then, within half-an-hour, strip naked in the woods and behave with such complete abandon? Which was the real Martita? Had the exhibition at the revival meeting been so much spoof? Had she been enjoying herself, putting on a cynical act? Then I heard again her clear voice singing,

"I'm living — on the mountain — underneath a cloudless sky," and I saw again her look of rapt devotion as she listened to the prayers, and I could not believe that such a young (I would not say "innocent") girl could be such an accomplished actress.

I asked myself again, How could anyone do it? and then realised the explanation lay within myself. For I had done much the same. True, I had not entered into the spirit of the revival meeting as unreservedly as Martita had, for these displays of emotion embarrassed me. Then I remembered what she had said,

"Don't be so worried, Steve. Let yourself go."

The realisation came to me that that was the clue to Martita 's character. She was a child of moods and emotions. She surrendered to the experiences of the moment. She let herself go. There was nothing incongruous or inconsistent about her, after all. She just accepted life as it came, enjoyed whatever offered...and lived. It was I who was afraid of life, who drew back from its experiences, who was nervous about what other people would think.

To all the turbulent events of the evening was added this flash of self-revelation. Ideas, memories, reassessments, introspection, surged chaotically through my tired mind all the way home. I let myself in through the back door, took off my shoes quietly in the kitchen, and crept up to bed, thankful to be spared encounters with my family. I thought I would find it difficult to get to sleep with so much to think about, but I must have dived into oblivion the moment my head hit the pillow.

Although I shrank from discussing the events of Sunday evening with my family, I could not resist asking my mother, when I got her alone, what she thought of Martita. She gave me a queer, sidelong look,

"She's a very remarkable girl," she said.

Then she added,

"But I don't think you'll hold her, Steve. She's not for you."

I had to smile. This, of course, was where my mother was mistaken. I had held her tighter than my mother could ever have dreamt of, and she was, beyond all argument, mine.

Oddly enough, Aunt Maria used the same adjective to describe Martita next time I saw her.

"That's a remarkable girl you've taken up with, Steve," she commented.

My mind was elsewhere at that moment, and I had to collect my thoughts.

"Oh, you mean in chapel on Sunday night," I said. "Yes, but she has other sides to her character."

"I can believe that," said Aunt Maria, dryly.

My mind, which always needs time to adjust itself, was still at the chapel meeting.

"Did you know that hymn that she started up?"

"I've heard it,"

"It seemed appropriate, somehow."

"It suited your Uncle's mood."

Which brought me to the question I had been wanting to ask her ever since I heard of Uncle Walter's conversion.

"Aunt Maria, do you think that Uncle Walter has really found his treasure?"

"He thinks he has," said Aunt Maria. "And he's happy."

"But do you think that was the Secret of Elderberry Lane? Was that what Aunt Sarah meant?"

"What do you think?" she countered.

I reflected.

"No, I don't think it was. I don't think she had that in mind."

"Nor do I," admitted Aunt Maria.

Chapter Ten

The more I thought about it, the more attractive I found Martita's philosophy of life. I considered care-worn father, oppressed by mounting bills which he hoped to be able to meet after harvest, at my hard-working mother, at the other Nadderbourne farmers who, crushed by the Depression, were abandoning their outer fields and sacking their men, at the farm workers I knew, working long hours for thirty shillings a week, at Mr. Nutbeam at the shop, harassed by the need to extend lengthier and ever lengthier credit, at all the folk of this impoverished village, and I realised that the happiest people I knew were Martita and Uncle Walter. Both, it occurred to me, were basing their life on the text I had so often heard read from the chapel pulpit,

"Take therefore no thought for the morrow; for the morrow shall take thought for the things of itself. Sufficient unto the day is the evil thereof."

They were both taking things as they came, not worrying about the future but participating without reserve in the experiences of the day. (I must admit, though, that I hoped that Martita was continuing, as she assured me from time to time, to take sufficient thought for the future to ensure that our love-making would have no catastrophic results.)

Their philosophy was readily applicable in the season of harvest, which we now entered. All through the year we had been working and planning for this climax. The ploughing, harrowing, dung-carting, sowing, rolling, weeding, had all been undertaken with the distant day of reaping in mind. (And at this time it didn't occur to me, a youth of nineteen, to query what would have happened if we had indeed taken no thought for the future and had so declined to engage in any of these laborious jobs.) Now the period of forward planning was past. We lived only for the day, each one of which seemed a hundred hours long.

The horse-drawn binder cut the corn and threw out lines of sheaves on the stubbles. 'Hilers' followed it, picking up the sheaves and standing them into 'Hiles', or stooks. After a few days of drying, if the weather were fine we tossed the sheaves on to horse-drawn wagons and carted them to stack-yards, where they were built into ricks. Summarised like that, it sounds simple, but each operation went on for days, in field after field, and each called for considerable skill, as well as stamina.

I generally managed to slip home for a mid-day lunch, but it was a convention for tea to be brought to us in the fields by the womenfolk. At about four o'clock we would see them tramping along a field track, some with prams or push-chairs in which infants, intrigued by this unusual afternoon experience, shared the accommodation with baskets of sandwiches and cans of tea or stone jars of cider. Some walked with a can or basket in either hand, and some pushed bicycles, with their burdens suspended from the handlebars. At this welcome sight we knocked off work, and all sat under a rick or a stook of sheaves and picnicked. For parched harvesters there has never been a beverage like hot tea from milk-cans in a harvest–field on a torrid afternoon.

We had left home at nine o'clock that morning, after completing the farmyard chores. We did not expect to return until after dark – say, nine or ten o'clock. In those days we possessed no radio sets, and no daily papers were delivered to Nadderbourne. Our horizons were therefore the fields of Nadderbourne; our news, the local gossip retailed by the women who brought our tea, and even that was a chatty background to the all-important task of gathering the harvest before the autumn storms broke. We kept an eye on the south-western sky, from which rain-clouds might be expected to appear; we took note of the high, wispy cirrus clouds overhead, which generally betokened the approach of rain, twenty-four hours away; we watched the behaviour of the swallows (which skimmed low over the fields when rain was imminent), of spiders (inclined to peep out of their cobwebby lairs at the approach of rain), of rooks, which foraged far afield from their rookery when the weather was set fair, and of various other creatures of the countryside whom we thought had advance notice of changes in the weather.

Once Martita had discovered this routine she adapted herself to it with alacrity. Accepted, though initially with considerable reservations, by my mother, she took to calling at the house each afternoon to collect our tea. She and Mary Ann would harness our fat, overfed, pet pony, Sooty, to the trap and drive to whichever field happened to be the scene of our labours. They joined the chattering clan for the picnic tea and then would help with whatever task was on hand. Martita got on well with both the women and the men, admiring the babies of the former and chaffing the latter. She was a friendly soul and talked easily. Mary Ann adored her.

In the evenings, as the light was fading, I would leave someone else to take the horses home and I would walk across the fields with Martita, hand in hand, pausing for an interlude of love under a hile or in the tall, sere August grasses or in an uncut cornfield or whatever alternative cover offered. Or sometimes when the last loaded wagon of the day was going back to the farmyard, as sometimes happened, we would ride atop it, in a snug nest of my making. I can still relive those swaying, jolting rides, in our lofty eyrie high above the berry-clad hawthorn hedgerows and level with the tall, rustling elms, branches of which occasionally brushed against us – both of us spent and weary with hard work yet still able to thrill at each other's proximity. What an idyllic life it was!

Two of the field then attached to our farm were Stony Lawn and Vincent's, so on several occasions our evening ride on a tall wagon took us along Elderberry Lane. Lying flat on the sheaves and peeping over the edge of the load we had a bird's-eye view of the landmarks in this story – White Ox Pond, Sarah Kennett's ruined cottage, Ensell's Garden, Noah's Close, Austin's, Halfpenny, Spallix and Uncle Walter's little farmstead. Once or twice we passed Uncle Walter himself, still leaning on a gate or sauntering slowly along the lane, while his cows grazed on the grass verge.

"I wonder what the Secret of the Lane really is," I remarked idly, one evening, "and whether we shall ever know."

And I sat up and let my eye follow its winding, white, gravelly course westwards to the keeper's cottage and Hobbit's Copse.

"Does it matter?" said Teeta, and drew me back down to the cosiness of our sheaf nest.

I made no attempt at resistance, particularly as we were just turning the corner and would shortly be passing the Vickary Farm. My conscience was still uneasy about Helen.

One disconnected episode of the harvest period has a slight bearing on this narrative. As often happened towards the end of summer, the ponds ran low and we were forced to draw water from the wells for our livestock, – a laborious and unpopular task. Our sheep were then grazing in Austin's, – a field of permanent grass, used also by the village cricket club as a playing field. The idea occurred to my father that the well in Aunt Sarah's neglected garden would be a more convenient source of water for the sheep than the more distant one at the farm. So he sent one of the men down to remove the covering (it had been boarded up to prevent children from falling in) and repair the well-crib and windlass. Joby, old Mrs. Endicott's mongol son, used to spend several hours a day there, drawing buckets of water.

A short cut from the farm to Stony Lawn and adjacent fields lay across Austin's and through the old garden. One morning, when I was going that way with my brother Stan and old Jimmy Jarman, my mongrel terrier, Bouncer, went racing on ahead, having spotted a young rabbit, and fell down the well. Joby, who could do a straightforward job like drawing water but was unreliable about anything else, had neglected to close the lid.

There was a booming roar and a splash as Bouncer hit the dark water in the depths. Uncle Walter who was with his cows in the lane just outside the garden gate, hear the commotion and came ambling over to join our alarmed group peering down the well. I called, and when the echoes had died away I could hear splashing down below. Evidently Bouncer had survived the fall and was struggling to keep afloat.

"Let's let the bucket down!" I exclaimed, "Perhaps he'll scramble in."

And I hurried to manipulate the windlass for that purpose, though paying out the rope gently, so that the bucket should not knock out the dog as it landed. Uncle Walter made a helpful suggestion.

"Run along to my place, son," he ordered Stan, "and fetch a flashlight."

Stan raced off immediately.

After the bucket had struck the bottom, I allowed it to remain floating for a few minutes and then started to haul it up. But it was useless. After turning the windlass a few rounds I could tell from the weight, or rather, the lack of it, that Bouncer was not clinging to it.

"It baint no use," commented Jimmy Jarman. "Somebody'll have to go down."

We wound the bucket to the top, a task which allowed sufficient time for Stan to come back with an electric torch. It was only a small one – a flat model of the type which we were accustomed to get as a minor present from a Christmas tree and we called a "flashlight" – but it would serve. Switching it on and contriving to hold it in one hand while gripping the wire rope like a clam, I stood in the bucket over the black pit and told the others to lower away.

"Gently now," I called, as I disappeared into the depths.

It was not an experience I would willingly repeat. The bucket swayed under my weight, tilting this way and that and bumping me against the slippery sides of the hole. The torch kept failing, its battery sliding about in a case too large for it. The blackness enveloped me as I frantically shook it, and the only light came from a circle, about the size of the Harvest Moon, far above me, against which the heads and shoulders of Uncle Walter, Jimmy Jarman and Stan were silhouetted. Splashings down below indicated that Bouncer was still gallantly keeping afloat.

Presently I arrived. The bucket, titling even more as it received support from the water, nearly tipped me out, and Bouncer, yelping with relief, frantically pawed my legs. Fortunately, at that moment the torch chose to come to life again. I was able to see what I was doing as I bent down to grab the dog by the collar and haul him out of the black water. I tucked his wet body under one arm, kept my feet planted as firmly as possible in the swaying bucket and yelled,

"Haul away."

As we started to ascend, Bouncer, struggling, knocked the torch out of my hand, and it fell into the water, extinguishing itself. There, I presume, it still is, waiting to greet some archaeologist in the distant future. Its loss left me less burdened than I would otherwise have been, and I settled down to the long ascent, determined that, whatever happened, I must not relax my grip on either the rope or Bouncer. With the extra weight, the bucket swung like a pendulum, bruising my elbow and knees as it bumped them against the sides. At the lower levels the well had been roughly finished, with many a projecting angle of chalk or flint. I seemed to hit every one, and some of them were dislodged and went crashing against the bucket and then down into the water below.

My arms were aching almost to breaking point and my knees were trembling uncontrollably when at last we reached the surface. Waiting hands reached for me and the dog. With inexpressible relief I found myself lying on the grass by the well–crib. Bouncer, likewise trembling, recovered himself first and shook himself, spraying me with water.

"Be ee all right?" asked Jimmy Jarman, anxiously.

"I reckon so," I panted.

"I lost the torch, though," I added, to Uncle Walter. "It fell into the water. I'm sorry."

But Uncle Walter was peering into the bucket.

"Hey! Look at this! he exclaimed, extracting something from it.

He held up a lump of wet chalk, in which gleamed and sparkled small nuggets of a shining yellow substance!

"Gold!" he murmured, reverently.

"Gold?" we echoed.

I struggled to my knees, and the others rushed over to inspect his find. When, at last, it was my turn to see and handle the rock, I was as impressed and excited as the others. The nuggets were embedded in the chalk, in a kind of lode. Doubtless, if we could find the place from which the chalk had been detached as it fell into the bucket, there would be more.

"We've found a gold-mine!" shouted Stan.

We closed the lid of the well and, as Uncle Walter would not allow anyone else to hold "his" treasure for more than half-a-minute, we all went hurrying along to his cottage. I've never seen Uncle Walter move so fast. The cows could safely be left to graze in Elderberry Lane, as usual. This was no break in routine for them.

Aunt Maria, when we burst into her kitchen, took the news calmly. She was allowed to take the chalk with its golden burden in her hands and inspect it.

"Hmm," she said. "You'd better let your father see it, Steve."

So we went racing up the road to the farm, – all of us, Jimmy Jarman panting to keep up – and were lucky enough to find my father about to set out for the harvest-field. Eagerly, we told him what had happened and showed him our treasure. He turned it over several times and then pronounced the verdict of deflation and disappointment.

"Aye," he said. "'Tis gold all right, but fools' gold! You find it in the chalk sometimes, especially deep down, when you're digging wells. Its proper name is 'Iron pirates', or something like that, I believe."

"Is it worth anything?" we asked, hopefully.

"Not a ha'penny!"

So that was that. I looked up the word in an encyclopaedia when I had time and, after a long search made more difficult because of the pronunciation of the word, found it under "Iron Pyrites". It was just as my father had said.

Fools' Gold or not, however, it was sufficient to set Uncle Walter treasure-hunting again. On his daily walks with the cows he pieced together to his own satisfaction the several discoveries that had been made during the summer.

There was the king with the golden helmet who had been buried in

Golden Cap Tump. The archaeologist had said that he probably lived hereabouts. There must have been a settlement somewhere by Elderberry Lane. And where did the gold come from? Uncle Walter argued that it was probably found in the same spot; that that was why the settlement was made there in the first place.

A settlement must have water. Ignoring the Coxenbourne, which would have been conveniently situated for any village in or near White Ox Acres, he decided that the water must come from wells. And it was while digging wells that the villagers had discovered gold – real gold and not this trashy Fools' Gold.

So there had been treasure in Elderberry Lane, after all, and now he knew what he must do to find it. He had to decide where that settlement was, to find those wells, and then to dig out the gold.

Uncle Walter treasure-hunting again became a familiar sight to all who passed along Elderberry Lane. This time, though, he had company. Old Jimmy Jarman, too aged and feeble to do much sustained work on the farm though willing to 'hile' or hoe for a few hours a day, had picked up many accomplishments during his long life, including the ability to dowse. Now he attached himself to Uncle Walter. One could see the two old men pottering around White Ox Acres or one of the other fields adjacent to the lane. Jimmy would be striding backwards and forwards, his forked hazel twig grasped between his extended hands. Every now and then the end of the twig would twist up and hit him in the chest. Excitement would follow, as he checked on his findings from every direction, endeavouring to determine just where the underground spring lay. Uncle Walter would mark its indicated course with sticks. Then the two of them would probe the surface with a long, thin metal rod, trying to locate a spot which, though allowing easy penetration by the rod, suggested previous digging. That way they hoped to discover an ancient well, and as the autumn wore on the fields became pock-marked by their excavations. As they confined their explorations to the farther, uncultivated fields, no-one interfered with them.

I asked Aunt Maria one day what she thought of the new development.

"Oh, he's happy enough," was her verdict. "It helps to keep his mind occupied. He was getting a bit bored."

Chapter Eleven

Nadderbourne's traditional sabbatarianism had a therapeutic effect on our lives. By Saturday night we were ready for a break. To have kept up the pace, seven days a week, for the six or eight weeks of harvest would have been asking too much. Undoubtedly in a stormy summer the effort would have been demanded, however, if it had not been for the religious taboo – call it superstition if you like – vetoing work on Sundays. Even agnostic farmers, though sorely tempted, would never flout convention.

For the Maidments, the Vicaries, the Pendles, and the Nutbeams and the other pillars of the chapel the temptation was less powerful, in that the chapel kept them too busy on Sundays. For them it was not a matter of sitting idly at home, frustratedly watching the fine weather being wasted; they were fully occupied with their religious duties. As for me, like all teenagers I was in rebellion against the conventions of the preceding generation, but to a fairly modest degree, for I was not really the stuff of which rebels are made. We compromised at a once-a-day attendance at a chapel service, leaving the rest of the Sabbath free.

Martita was now a frequent visitor to my home for Sunday tea. As a matter of fact, we fell into a routine whereby she came on alternate Sundays. On the intervening ones, I went up to Princedun House. Yes, we had reached the stage when I was accepted there as Martita's friend,...though the acceptance amounted to less than I imagined.

On the first occasion I was doubly uncomfortable, partly through apprehension and partly through having donned a tie and jacket on a scorching afternoon. I climbed the imposing steps to the vast Gothic porch, sent the echoes reverberating by my tentative tattoo on the massive knocker, and was admitted by a dignified butler. Martita came running to meet me and led me though the house to the garden on the other side. We didn't see another soul.

It was the most casual household imaginable. I soon realised how it was that Martita could stay out till what my mother would have considered unreasonable hours for her daughter, with no questions asked. People came and went just as they pleased. There was no formal tea-time, of the kind I had expected and dreaded. About half-past four, when we felt hungry, we sauntered into the drawing-room and there found sandwiches daintily arranged on a tray, with tea in a silver tea-pot. We helped ourselves to what we wanted and went outside to eat, seated by the lily-pool.

Martita's mother was in London, then in Paris. I did not meet her until, I think, my fourth visit. She then eyed me briefly but without, it seemed to me, noticing me much. Her mind, I think, was elsewhere. I had the impression that she did not exactly approve of me but that it was a matter of little consequence. Martita could doubtless look after herself, and that if she chose to spend her summer with me, that was her affair. Mrs Vannecke had her own summer programme, and, whatever else it involved, Princedun House featured in it only as a convenient base.

I met Lord Crewkerne more frequently. He would amble in and out of the rooms, usually followed by two black retrievers.

"Let me see, you're Maidment's son," he said, on our first encounter. "How's the harvest going?"

He had a languid, casual air, but I think this was a conventional pose. He was very knowledgeable about farming, and about Nadderbourne affairs.

Lady Crewkerne was likewise placid and vague. She always extended a friendly greeting and would then launch into a monologue about whatever was on her mind, such as plans for the rose garden, or something she had read in the daily paper (where she had an advantage over me, who never saw a daily paper), or a music festival at Wilcester, or gossip about the domestic affairs of neighbouring estate-owners. I soon realised that she was just as interested in the idiosyncracies of her neighbours as my mother was, only she operated on a county rather than a village basis. Half the time I had no idea of what or whom she was talking about, but that didn't matter. She just liked talking, and if I happened to be present I was a convenient stooge.

Now and again she would pose a question or make a remark which suggested she was not as vague about me and my background as she generally seemed to be. Once she asked, suddenly, and apropos of nothing that had gone before,

"Does the *Ornithogalum pyrenaicum* still grow by Elderberry Lane?"

The question floored me completely. I had no idea what *Ornithogalum pyrenaicum* might be, so I temporised and said I would find out. As she was obviously referring to a plant, the best person to ask would have been Helen, but that was an impossibility. One day, though, I happened to meet Miss Simpkins, who, in response to my question, said brightly,

"Ah yes, the Spiked Stars of Bethlehem. Yes, there's a little colony in the hedge by Nimitty. They're probably over by now, though. They bloom in July."

I remembered to pass on the information to Lady Crewkerne, who, when she had adjusted her mind to what I was talking about, said,

"They often grow near the site of old gardens. Cottagers used to gather the young shoots and sell them as asparagus. Tell me, what do you think of this little composition Charles bought the other day. It's of the Piazza del Campo in Siena, and it's by an artist named Arturo Santerno, as far as I can make out."

Completely out of my depth, I examined the painting and tried to make intelligent comments. My subconscious mind, however, made a note of the fact that there had probably once been a garden and therefore a house in Nimitty. That could, just possibly, have a bearing on the Secret of the Lane.

Harvest dragged on, impeded by frequent periods of rain, for it was a stormy summer. We grew weary of turning sodden sheaves to dry, knowing that when that aim was realised we would have to race the clouds to get them stacked in ricks before they received another soaking. It was frustrating work. The early joy had fled from harvest, but we stuck grimly to our task. There was, indeed, no alternative. The older men accepted the struggle philosophically as a familiar pattern of events. The cycle of the country year was for them a campaign in which the enemy was the weather, aided by pests and diseases and all the hostile forces of nature, to reach its culmination annually in the Battle of the Harvest, which, somehow, had to be won.

This later phase of harvest dealt mostly with the barley crop, which is unpleasant stuff to handle. The sheaves are light in weight and short, and the straw soft, but barley has prickly awns (called by us "barley ailes") which break off at touch and cling to one's clothes and persons. They lodge in underwear, wriggle into crevices and make one itchy and irritable. Having had one experience of loading a wagon with these deplorable bundles, Martita preferred to keep her feet on the ground and to lead the horse. I wished I could do the same. Sometimes, when the rains were pretty frequent, she missed coming to the harvest-field, and I looked in vain for her all day. My mood then matched the grey, dismal canopy that veiled the sky. And sometimes she would find us in the fields and, after keeping us company for a few minutes, would drift away to the hedges to gather blackberries.

For the flowers of the hedgerows were almost over, and the time of berries had arrived. The petals of the dog roses had fallen long ago, to be replaced by reddening hips. The hawthorn bushes had shed their perfumed flowers and were now bending under the weight of red clusters of haws. Deep purple clusters of elder berries hung from the larger bushes, from which many were stripped by village housewives, bent on making wine. It was also a good year for blackberries, which tempted the fruit pickers to the brambles festooning every unkempt hedge, the biggest and best always tantalisingly just out of reach. Elderberry Lane was flaunting its own harvest. Farther down the lane, the hazel bushes shading it from the edge of Hobbit's Copse were bearing a good crop of nuts, and the big beech trees were loaded with sufficient beech-mast to keep all the pigeons, jays and squirrels in the district satisfied till Christmas. The giant maple tree in Austin's likewise bore of heavy crop of winged seeds – a sight which I found mildly frustrating, for it seemed to me that they ought to be useful for something, although, as far as I knew, they were not.

"Well, me bwoy, we shall soon be able to shout, 'Well ploughed, well sowed, well harred, well mowed, and all safely carted into the barn wi' nary a load throwed, hip-hip-hooray,' said Old Jimmy Jarman one Saturday afternoon in Pig Close.

It was the old Harvest Shout, which we no longer used at Nadderbourne, though the old chaps remembered it. It was the prelude to the Harvest Home Feast, which had been lost in the bleak years of the war and the depression. Still, the sentiment was valid. Even after this laborious, exasperating harvest the feeling of relief at seeing the end in sight was mixed with elation. The task was nearly complete. Only the seven acres of barley remaining in Pig Close to be carted on Monday, and then we could resume something nearer a normal existence. We would even be able to adhere to the provisional arrangements for the annual local Darby – a cricket match between Nadderbourne and our traditional rivals at Shuffley – on the following Saturday.

It was with a more light-hearted step than usual, a feeling akin to that which I used in the last days of term at school before breaking up for the holidays, that I walked along Elderberry Lane on the Sunday afternoon, climbing the gate at the junction of Hobbit's Copse and Verngrove and taking the woodland path. It was my turn to have tea at Princedun House.

Martita met me in the nightjar clearing. I was rather surprised at this, as she usually let me come right up to the House before putting in an appearance, but I was delighted to see her, and we kissed.

When we broke apart, however, I realised that she looked grave, and so asked,

"Why so solemn?"

"I don't think you'd better come to the House today, Steve," she said. "We're in disgrace."

"Eh? Why? How?"

"Somebody's been watching us, and they've told my uncle."

My heart gave a great leap of apprehension. In far less time than it takes to set this down, my mind raced over the details of the numerous uninhibited encounters Teeta and I had enjoyed here in the woods, and I flushed alternately hot and cold.

"Who?"

"Think it was the keeper."

Henry Upshot. It *would* be.

"What did he see?"

"I don't know. But he's told my uncle something, and there's a distinct coldness in the air up at the House. It's definitely anti-Steve."

"Yes. It would be," I agreed. "What's going to happen?"

"Nothing for the moment, I guess. I don't think they know too much. There's been no outright prohibiition on our meetin'. But I guess it would be better if you didn't come to tea."

I agreed with that.

"My mother comes back from Le Tropez on Wednesday, and I guess they're waitin' until then."

"Yes, I expect that's it. Oh, Teeta, I do hope you won't get into trouble."

"Aw, it can't be all that bad. If it comes to a showdown, it's my word against this godammed keeper's and I can swear blind he's mistaken. Still, I guess it's bound to make them careful about little Martita in the future."

That seemed logical. And then we went on to face the problem that we had been resolutely consigning to the attics of our mind all the summer, – that the time must come when Martita would have to return to the States. It could only be a matter of weeks now, at the most, before we must part. We let our thoughts run over fantastic possibilities, such as eloping or my emigrating to California, but for me, whose horizons were still bounded by the fields of Nadderbourne, they all seemed as absurd as a flight to the moon, and even Martita, who was much more sophisticated and knowledgeable, dismissed them as impracticable. We would have to wait and see what Mrs. Vannecke decreed when she came home on Wednesday.

So, with the future so obscure, we could only take refuge in the present. Seeking a forest of fern so situated that it would be almost impossible for a spying keeper to approach us unawares, we sank into its cool depths, shaped a nest around our bodies and surrendered ourselves to the ecstasy of what would, in our memory, seem nothing more than a dream

We stayed there as long as we dared – until, in fact, Teeta felt that a longer delay would lead to awkward enquiries back at Princedun House. We clung to each other, running our fingers over the curves of each other's bodies, as though it were imperative for us to imprint every detail on the archives of memory. We kissed, and looked long into each other's eyes. Then, reluctantly, we dressed, and Teeta walked slowly towards the woods that encompassed the glade. She half-turned for a moment, offering me a look of agonising appeal, as I stood deep-rooted as one of the oaks that overhung our bower of ferns. Then she started running, stumbling like a stoated rabbit, along the last reach of Elderberry Lane that led to Princedun, and so vanished amid the trees.

With an aching head and a confusion of thoughts, I made my way eastwards along narrow woodland paths, rather than westwards in the direction of Nadderbourne. I could not face going home yet. Eventually I emerged from the forest on to Juniper Down, where I disturbed an assembly of stone curlew , gathering in preparation for migration. They took wing and sped away, a token, I felt, of what Martita must shortly do. There was no comfort for me, even in the familiar world of nature. I sat on the stone parapet of Puck Bridge for some time, watching the chiffchaffs or willow warblers (I did not know which) stoking up with insects among the willow trees of the Coxenbourne, preparatory, too, to their flight to Africa. In a world of free movement, only I, restless and rebellious, remained shackled, tied by the conventions of this rural society into which I had been born. Ahead stretched the long, austere vista of the dark months, their gloom unrelieved by blossom or song, until, far beyond the distant watershed of the years, the flowers bloomed again and the birds returned full of enthusiasm for another season of mating and fulfilment. And that thought at last gave me a measure of peace, or at least a focus of hope for the future. The eventual coming of spring was, I knew from experience, inevitable even though often delayed, and perhaps the return of Martita, as she had promised, could equally be relied on. For she had sworn, if by any means possible, to come to Princedun again in the floowing summer. By then we would both be a year older and might meet with less opposition when we raised with our families the question of becoming engaged.

I did not return home till after eight o'clock, not wishing to admit to my mother that I had not been to Princedun to tea. Even so, she said,

"Hm, you're early tonight, my son."

I waited until she went out to shut up the fowl-house in the orchard and then slipped into the pantry. The bread and cheese which I found there and subsequently ate in the barn both lined my stomach and gave me a less gloomy outlook on life, for a growing lad cannot be expected to endure simultaneously a harrowing of the soul and the loss of a meal without experiencing some deterioration of his mental attitude. In short, by the time I had also managed to acquire, without being observed, a brimming mug of cider I was feeling decidedly more cheerful. I went to bed and slept like a two-year-old.

More often than not, our cricket matches; played in Austin's, were watched by the merest handful of spectators, chiefly old–age pensioners, one or two mothers with families of small children who made themselves a nuisance to the out-fielders, and the wives or girl-friends of a few of the players. We were often so low in supporters that the batting side had to supply two umpires. The annual conflict with Shuffley, however, provided a notable contrast. The visiting side was sure to send a contingent of supporters, on bikes, by horse-and-trap and, latterly, by car, which made it obligatory for the home crowd to turn out, too. A dozen or so village housewives were kept busy all the afternoon preparing a tea in the schoolroom for approaching a hundred people. It was the grand climax of the cricket season, just as harvest was of the cycle of the farm.

We played alternately at Nadderbourne and Shuffley, and this year was the turn of Nadderbourne. The seemingly endless procession of rain-clouds from the south-west had at last been deflected – to Scotland or somewhere else where, it was to be hoped, they needed them more than we did, – and the sun, visible again at last, was beaming down with the enthusiasm of a horse let out into a green meadow after a winter in stable. The sheep had been transferred to a new pasture, and the cricket pitch in Austin's swept clear of their droppings (for they loved to lie on the smooth pitch, in preference to the rougher outfield, at nights and manure it when they woke up to feed in the mornings). Stan and I had spent most of the previous day clearing away cow-pats and cutting clumps of nettles and thistles in the outfield. The setting for the contest was perfect.

Shuffley won the toss and batted first. Like most village cricket teams, we relied on the speed rather than the cunning of our fast bowlers, who launched a battering attack that made our wicket-keeper, Tim Mather, retreat to about twenty yards behind the stumps. But the Shuffley batsmen were doughty opponents, well experienced in that sort of cricket. In particular Bill Keevil, the Shuffley schoolmaster, soon took the measure of the bowling and scored pretty freely with leg glides and cuts past fine slip, thus allowing the bowler to do most of the work for him. A gentle touch to balls hurled at that speed was sufficient to deflect them to the boundary.

We got him at last, caught behind wicket, but not before he had scored 56. Nobody had ever scored a century in any village cricket match that could be remembered, and a half-century was a notable achievement. The rest of the Shuffley batsmen backed him up reasonably well. We tried six bowlers, had a gruelling afternoon in the field, and eventually polished off the innings with a run-out at about half-past four. The Shuffley score was 126.

In the hall the tea-urn, of polished brass, stood on the edge of the stage, so that the busy witresses could replenish their tea-pots with a minimum of effort. It was flanked by trays of sandwiches (incorporating lettuce, ham, cucumber or scrambled egg) and of cakes, including Mrs. Pendle's noted lardy and seed cakes. On a table in the centre of the stage, flanked by jars of Michaelmas daisies and chrysanthemums and with a large Union Jack as a backcloth, stood the keg of cider which would be the trophy of the winning team.

The rule for cricket teas was that the players,umpires and score-keepers ate free of charge. Anyone else was welcome to join in, at a charge of a shilling. For this annual jamboree, however, there was no fixed fee but a collection, which was considered to be a more profitable method of tapping latent support. It could be expected to yield several ££s, which was divided between the two clubs. Each of the two captains made a speech, the captain of the home side welcoming the guests and the visiting captain responding. Then the two of them went around the trestle tables with their caps, ours red with a yellow badge, the Shuffley colours green and red. Altogether a pleasant, social occasion, marred for me by the absence of Martita, whom I had hoped would be there but whom I had not seen since Sunday.

After our strenuous afternoon in the field, the evening promised to be less exacting, except for the batsmen during their stint at the wicket. We had no pavilion but had lined up wooden benches, borrowed from the hall, by the hedge along the western side of the meadow, dividing it from the field we called Halfpenny. There the spectators were sheltered from such breeze as there was, winnowing in from the south-west, and also had the declining sun behind them. Some of the better-off villagers had brought canvas deck-chairs for their wives, and some sat in traps and carts.

Nadderbourne had a disasterous start to its innings, losing two men for only five runs. The third man went with only 16 on the scoreboard, but then we rallied. John Mellish, Mr Vickary's carter, settled down to a dogged, defensive innings, while Les Nutbeam, old Joseph Nutbeam the shopkeeper's nephew, set about the bowling with a lack of respect that soon had the spectators cheering. There was considerable muttering when the Shuffley umpire gave him out, l.b.w.. "Never in this world!" "Put on yer glasses, man!" "Thik ball wur damned near a wide!" chorussed the critics. But they soon cheered up when Oscar Batten, the landlord's son from the Old Bell, carried on where Les Nutbeam had left off and lambasted the bowling all over the field. Boundaries simply flowed from his bat, and he smote one magnificent six that sent the spectators scattering, the ball landing with a resounding thud on the floor of a cart, fortunately empty of people. It was too scintillating to last. Attempting to repeat that mighty stroke, Oscar mis-hit and propelled the ball into the safe hands of the Shuffley wicket-keeper. Now it was my turn. Fully equipped with pads and gloves, a resplendent figure in white (although I say it myself), I marched out to take my place in the arena. For as long as I could hold Shuffley bowling at bay, I was the champion of Nadderbourne. Why, oh why, was Martita not there to see my hour of glory? if that is what it was to be – there was always the chance that my wicket would be shattered by the first ball. The score stood at 86. 41 more runs to win.

Like all village youngsters I had started my cricketing career by knocking a ball about in the school playground as soon as I was big enough to hold a bat. I had first played for the village team when fifteen, batting at No.11 and fielding long-stop. From that lowly base I had worked my way up and was batting now in about the middle of the order. My superiors tended to regard me as a promising youngster, who could play useful cricket on his "on" days, when he could restrain himself from taking foolish risks. Today I resolved to keep myself well under control. No wild slashing at balls outside the off stump. With 41 runs still to score and no recognised batsmen behind me in the tail-end, I had a heavy responsibility.

Shuffley had a more sophisticated bevy of bowlers than ours. In particular they had Ivor Burge, the postman, a man of mature years (he must have been fifty) who, no longer able to hurtle the balls down the pitch at breakneck speed, relied instead on guile. He kept an immaculate length, dead on the middle stump, and flighted the ball in the air. When it hit the pitch it more often than not proceeded in a straight line, but every now and again it swerved to the offside. The first ball I received was one of these breakers, and it nearly had me. I drew my bat back only just in time, or I would have deflected an easy catch into the hands of one of the waiting slips.

For the first over or two I groped and prodded, and my morale was not helped by the fall, at last, or John Mellish who, reaching forward to the fast bowler operating at the other end, was neatly stumped. Pat

Reynolds, under shepherd on Passmore's Farm, who came in next had a reputation as a slogger — a mighty hitter of all types of balls. He started off in fine style, with a couple of rather fluky fours off the fast bowler; then, in the next over, he set about Ivor Burge. He adopted the technique of advancing down the pitch to meet the ball and swiping it before ever it hit the ground. It needed for him to miss only one straight ball and his innings would have been over, but tonight he had his eye in and did not miss. Fours and sixes came apace, to the vociferous delight of the Nadderbourne supporters.

It could not last, of course. In due course, he mistimed a hit, sent the ball shooting almost vertically skywards and was out to a catch by the wicketkeeper. But in the meantime he had so discouraged Ivor Burge that the Shuffley captain had taken him off and called up another bowler. It was providential for me. Burge was the only bowler I feared. I reckoned I had the measure of the others.

After a couple of no-scoring batsmen, my brother Stan came in, and together we carried along the score nicely. We passed 100. Then 110. Then 120. I was now going well, but the tension building up in the spectators' seats under the hedge became so powerful that we sensed it in the middle of the field. The Nadderbourne clique cheered every ball that we kept away from our stumps, whether we scored or not. Another seven runs, and the match would be ours.

The Shuffley side had exhausted all their regular bowlers and were experimenting. The chap now trolling balls up to me was a newcomer – a Naval man on leave, so I understood, but he seemed fairly innocuous. The stuff he was sending up was straight and quite well pitched up, but not a bit tricky. I played a couple with a dead bat and then made up my mind just where I would place the next one, past square leg to boundary.

The ball was already being tossed to the bowler, in preparation for the next delivery, when I heard a car passing along Elderberry Lane, on the south boundary of Austin's. I glanced across and saw one of those big, imposing cars – Daimlers, I think they were – of which Princedun House had about half a dozen, sailing along towards the village. It had heavy luggage piled on the tail rack and the roof rack.

The driver looked to me very much like young David Sinclair-Penhammett, the Earl of Crewkerne's son and heir. In the back seat sat Mrs Vannecke, and by the driver's side I saw Martita waving frantically.

Before I could make up my mind whether, under the circumstances, it would be etiquette for me to wave back, the car had disappeared behind the big maple tree and the bowler was ambling up to the wicket. Talk about schizophrenia! One part of me wanted to drop my bat and go haring away over the field, in a vain chase after my love. Another was bitterly reproaching myself for not having the courage even to wave to her. A third was trying to decide whether to smash this ball to the boundary as planned or, in view of the unsettling interlude, to wait until the next one. I was still dithering when the ball arrived. It was slightly different in pace from the others. I played too soon, endeavouring to send it to square leg; and, instead, it popped off the edge of the bat to give a dolly catch to point.

The groan that went up from the Nadderbourne supporters was drowned by a yell of delight from the Shuffley crowd. Dejectedly, I walked away from the pitch, trailing my bat. I got an ovation, for I had scored 23 and had taken the score to within sight of victory, but mixed with the congratulations were cries of, "Whatever did ee do that for?" "Gawr, fancy fallin' for a ball like that!" "Wot wur ee thinkin', lad?"

One helpful old boy provided an alibi for me.

"Ar, the zun were in his eyes!" he declared.

Yes, that was as good an excuse as any.

"The sun was in my eyes," I remarked, as I threw down my bat under a bench and started to remove my pads.

The game was proceeding. Frank Dear, the blacksmith, was our last man, and one of whom not much was to be expected. Frank smote the ball like he hammered his anvil, but his eye, more acustomed to the gloom of the forge, was not attuned to the bright light of the autumn evening. His first flail-like stroke completely missed connecting with the ball. His second drove a long shot to near the long-on boundary and they ran two runs. The final ball of the over shattered all three of his stumps.

The match was over. We had come so near to succeeding and then failed. Shuffley had won, by 126 to 122.

There were congratulations and condolences, but I was in no mood for either. As soon as I decently could, I mumbled a few excuses about having to be gone, and, picking up my bat, I made my way across the meadows to home.

Changing, in my bedroom, from my white cricketing gear into the more usual grey flannels and jacket, I tried to analyse the situation. In the first place, I was ashamed of myself. I could have kicked myself for getting out to such a simple ball. I felt I had lost the match for Nadderbourne and disgraced myself in the eyes of half the parish. At nineteen I was still highly sensitive to public opinion.

Fighting memories of the match for pride of place in my thoughts, and speedily winning, was the conviction that Martita had gone away. Or rather, had been taken away. The car had been travelling away from Princedun House, in the direction of London. Her departure was the likely result of whatever it was that the Earl had heard about us. Nor did I like the idea of young David Sinclair-Penhammett, a chap of about my own age, as her travelling companion. I resented the thought of any other young man being near her.

And then there was my failure to return her last farewell wave. I had stood there, staring like a moron, not daring to do what any full-blooded man ought to have done. What a weak worm I was!

All this instrospection and self-abasement led to a general feeling of despondency. I felt like the Old Testament prophet, of whom I had often heard in chapel, who asked the Lord to leave him alone, as it was better for him to die than to live. I did not want to be questioned about the match, or about Martita (whose absence for a week must have been puzzling my mother), or, indeed, to talk to anyone about anything. Slinking downstairs, I crept out of a side-door and through the orchard.

I would take a lonely walk, to try to settle my chaotic thoughts. Not down Elderberry Lane, but in the opposite direction.

Chapter Twelve

It was as I feared. At the end of the following week I received a letter, with a London postmark, from Martita.

"My dear darling, sweetest Steve," it began, and then went on with such affectionate intimacies that I am not going to repeat them here. Some things must be forever private. The kernel of information in the diffuse epistle was that her mother had decided to take her to London and Paris before sailing for America. They would be embarking on an ocean liner at Cherbourg in about a fortnight's time. They would not be returning to Princedun this year, but she hoped to be able to persuade her mother to let her pay another visit next summer. A certain coldness in the atmosphere had made her feel she was in disgrace to a minor extent, but no specific charges had been levelled.

Well, that was something to be thankful for. A small crumb of comfort. Henry Upshot had evidently not carried a detailed report of our behaviour to the Earl, doubtless because he had not been near enough to see much of what went on. So perhaps the black marks against Martita would not be enough to keep her away permanently.

Meantime, she had gone from my life for at least a year, and I viewed the future disconsolately. It was not only that I loved Teeta; it was also a disruption of the pattern of my life. I had got used to her being around – a cheerful, chattering little partner, who could be trusted to have a novel, unconventional approach to almost anything. I had been accustomed to our evening strolls down Elderberry Lane and through the twilight woods. I could even now feel the roundness of her exquisitely-formed body and the warmth of her dainty, sensitive hands. I longed for the pressure of her hot lips on mine. All these delightful things I had become so used to, and now they were snatched from me.

I started going to Wilcester in the ramshackle bus (which had begun a regular Saturday and Sunday evening service about five years earlier). On Saturdays I would go to the music-hall – the old Wilcester Playhouse – or to the pictures; on Sundays, from force of habit, to a service in one of the city chapels or mission halls. Usually with myself, and always half-seeking company.

I was missing Teeta so much that at times I felt that almost any female company might soothe the ache. I looked tentatively at some of the brasher village girls – at big-busted, jolly Sue Farringdon, at Dolly Mellish, a sly furtive brunette who helped in the shop – but when it came to the pinch I recoiled from putting them in Martita's place. I wondered about Helen. Now with her I could have been at home and found some consolation, but she wouldn't even look at me. Not that I blamed her.

So the grey autumn wore on. The cycle of the year and of the farm took no account of my feelings. The land is a relentless slave-driver. Each task must be performed at the proper season, or the eventual punishment is severe. My father was a good farmer, who liked always to be ahead of schedule. The difference between a good farmer and a bad farmer is only a fortnight.

Immediately after the fields were cleared of harvest, portable fowl-houses were lodged on them, so that the hens could forage for their own living on the stubbles for six or eight weeks. It was a cheap way of keeping them at a time when most of them were moulting, anyway. The field that had been summer-fallowed we sowed with wheat. Over the stubble-field we spread dung and began burying it with the plough. We pulled mangolds and swedes and stored them in thatched clamps for winter use. I went with my father to Michaelmas sales and to the markets, buying here a second-hand binder, there a batch of fresh rams. The sheep were moved from the downs to turnip-fields, where new hurdle folds had to be pitched for them every day.

One of my usual tasks was to shut up the fowl–houses every evening after the hens had gone to roost, which they did within half-an-hour of sunset. On fine evenings it was a pleasant walk in the owl-light, to the accompaniment of eerie stone-curlew music and the occasional yelp of a fox. For much of the autumn the fowl-houses were in Stony Lawn and Vincent's fields on the side of Elderberry Lane towards Princedun Forest. It would have been so convenient for Martita to meet me there, and oh how I longed for her! I used to gaze at the shore of the ocean of trees and try to imagine her breaking out of their grasp and coming dancing over the fields to meet me...or rather, I tried not to imagine it. The visions came unbidden.

After the fowls had departed came the dung–carting and the ploughing, so, one way and another, much of the autumn was spent in these two fields. Often I was working alone, if one excepts the company of Bouncer and horses, and so had plenty of time for reflection and observation. With the innate perception of a country–bred lad I noted the signs of the season. The birds collected in autumn flocks, as though seeking the support of numbers in the ordeals that lay ahead.

Every afternoon, as the light began to fade, the starlings assembled in immense flocks in the elms that margined Elderberry Lane in the hedges of Spallix, Noah's Close and the Glebe Land. They came rushing in in tight-knit, hasty companies to join the chattering hordes already collected. Sometimes an entire flock would engage in marvellously synchronised acrobatics at high speed, twisting and spiralling like a kite's tail, as though they were one living entity rather than scores of independent units, and the noise they made was like that of sea breakers. And what was the trigger that eventually, when the last stragglers had arrived, caused the horde, as though at a signal from a conductor's baton, to cease their chatter at the same instant and immediately to rise in the air, like a cloud of locusts? They would then fly away eastwards, to their roost which I understood was in a copse on the other side of Nadderbourne

The peewits were also collecting in flocks on the stubble-fields and in the meadows. On an afternoon in early November I saw the first golden plover with them – just a dozen or so angular-winged visitors from the northern moors, retreating before the threat of winter. The fieldfares and redwings, those thrush-like birds from Scandinavia, had drifted in a fortnight earlier, the fieldfares appearing black and white against the clouds driven before an approaching gale. They called harshly, like the Vikings from the same lands who must once have passed this way, giving their name to Dane Hill.

With ample time to think, I let my imagination try to visualise those wild, bloodthirsty men who once went shouting along the lane. They must have done something more than just march along it, to have branded their name so firmly on a section of it that it endured for a thousand years. But what? So my thoughts ranged over the other men who had used the lane, and a long cavalcade of them paraded themselves, from the prehistoric men whose stone tools have been found in White Ox Acres to the wealthy Saxon chief who was buried in Golden Cap Tump to the school inspector whom I saw passing along on his way from Avonchurch to Nadderbourne School.

My eye fell on Aunt Sarah's ruined cottage, and I wondered whom she had seen in the lane during all the years she had lived by it. The Secret of the Lane came to the forefront of my mind again, and the sight of Uncle Walter strolling along with his cows twice a day kept it fresh. Though he was still never in a hurry, Uncle Walter had a new and absorbing interest. Jimmy Jarman's hazel twig had indicated an underground spring in Wells' Piece, and when he and Uncle had started to dig, sure enough they found they were on the site of an old well. With renewed zest they began to excavate. I used to walk over now and again to see how the work was going, and by the end of November they were down fifteen or sixteen feet. They had fixed up a racketty windlass and would take it in turns to clamber down a home-made, shaky ladder to dig, the other partner stationing himself to wind up bucketfuls of earth and rubbish. Mind you , even with this incentive, there was no obvious haste in the operation. More often than not I would find them smoking and discussing things as they leant on the well-crib, their tools idle on the ground.

With the Secret still in mind, I noted the people I myself saw in and around the lane that autumn, to consider whether they would offer any slight clue to what Aunt Sarah could have seen to set her on the track of the treasure.

For a few days in late September an abundant crop of mushrooms shot up in Austin's, Noah's Close and Spallix, and every morning I would see a galaxy of strange, stooping figures, shapeless as gnomes or Rodin's peasants, moving about in the mists. Sometimes only their heads and shoulders would be visible above the white vapours, sometimes it would be their feet and legs which would be hidden by a lagoon of gossamer. Mary Ann and Tom were generally deputed to represent our family in gathering the bonus harvest of the meadows, and were sometimes up in time for us to have fresh-plucked mushrooms with our eggs and bacon for breakfast – a truly delectable feast.

Also in September a party of guns from Princedun drove the Nadderbourne fields for partridges. I was spreading dung in Stony Lawn at the time and moved to the side of the field to give them an uninterrupted drive. They advanced in a long line strung right across the field, sportsman and beater alternately at intervals about twenty yards. The Earl himself was on the right wing and passed within five yards of where I stood waiting by the hedge. He gave me a brief nod but with no sign that he recognised me as anything more than one of the farmhands which were to him part of the normal rural scenery. The guns killed several brace in Stony Lawn, I remember, partridges being far more numerous then than they are now.

In October the Earl's attention naturally turned to pheasants. This, of course, was woodland sport rather than shooting in the open fields. The guns were stationed in glades and rides, such as the nightjar clearing by Elderberry Lane. I could hear the cannonade but saw nothing of the drive except old Billy Mellish, who was stationed as "stop" in Vincents. He had to patrol alongside the Deer Leap, banging the bushes with a long stick and making a noise whenever he heard a pheasant approaching. The idea was to keep the birds in the woods and to prevent them from escaping over the open fields. Old Billy was not very active and spent most of the day sitting on a bank with his pipe in his mouth. I saw him again as dusk was creeping over the countryside, trudging homeward after collecting his day's wages up at the House. With a few furtive glances, he retraced his steps over the beat he had been patrolling during the day and darted from time to time into the wood. He emerged, stuffing something into the capacious pockets of his long, shapeless overcoat. I reckon he picked up as least five pheasants. All day long he had marked where dead and wounded birds had fallen, and, with a lifetime's experience as a poacher, had returned unerringly to retrieve them. The four shillings he received from the head keeper was a minor portion of his day's takings.

In November the hunt spent a day around Nadderbourne, meeting on the Wilcester side of the Princedun Estate but finding their way into our fields by the early afternoon. Ploughing in Stony Lawn, I could hear the horn calling far away over Addle Down. Then a fox came slinking down the side of the hedge between Stony Lawn and Vincent's and crossed the lane into the Glebe Land. About ten minutes later a chap in a red jacket, on a big white horse, galloped over from Ship Pennings and, reining in, called,

"Hey, you! Have you seen the fox?"

Being young and never having given much thought to such matters, I automatically told him, pointing out the course the fox had taken. Nowadays I would have sent him in the opposite direction. He urged his horse forward and went off without a word.

These were occasional items in the autumn pageant of the countryside. More regularly, indeed with the utmost regularity, I saw Bob Mould and Sid Crendle, the woodmen, returning from their day's stint in the forest. They must have plodded down Elderberry Lane on their way to the woods in the early morning while I was still at the farmyard, but I saw them most afternoons, around sunset, homeward bound with their rush baskets slung over their shoulders and their billhooks in their hands.

Bob and Sid were survivals. A generation or two earlier perhaps a third of the working population of Nadderbourne found employment in the woods throughout autumn and winter. They were self-employed. At the end of summer Bob and Sid would interview the Earl of Crewkerne's agent and bargain for an acre each of underwood in the forest. For a small sum they would acquire the right to cut the hazel, sapling ash and other underwood in the oak coppices. These trees, after being cut, sent up clusters of shoots from their stubs. The shoots grew into tall, straight rods and were considered ready for cutting after about eight years. Bob and Sid would fashion them into sheep hurdles, bean-rods, clothes'-props, pea-sticks, sheep-cribs, wood faggots for burning and a number of other articles for domestic or farm use. At least, Bob concentrated on making hurdles; Sid, who was less skilled, did the rougher jobs. One of their first tasks at the beginning of their autumn work was to erect a little shed in a sheltered corner of their woodland block. Around it, as they cut their wood, they built a barricade of untreated brushwood and, later, of wood faggots, providing a shelter from every wind except the south. On wet days they could thus work in the dry; on fine days, their encampment was a sun–trap.

On a Sunday afternoon in November I wandered along the woodland sector of Elderberry Lane and came to the underwood workers' enclosure. It was in a block of woodland next to the nightjar glade, and they had made a path to it through the fern where only a few weeks earlier Martita and I had embraced. But already the bracken was as golden as a field of ripe wheat and was as good as dead. Soon it would be flat as a stubble-field, its brittle fronds trodden into the debris of the woodland floor.

So time inexorably obliterated the tangible background to our summer love affair, just as, down in Grove End Fields, the straw rick which held our secret cavern was being dismantled to provide litter for the cattle and pigs. Soon nothing would remain but memory.

One day in October I noticed a strange figure plodding along the lane towards Nadderbourne, and, as I was working near the field gate of Stony Lane, I paused to watch it pass. It was a stumpy little Italian organ-grinder, pushing a barrel-organ on top of which perched a forlorn-looking monkey. The man greeted me in a language which I did not understand, and I replied with a "Good Afternoon". Soon afterwards I heard the strains of his jerky music from the village street.

I had seen this Italian before. He used to come to Nadderbourne most years in autumn, visiting us on a round of villages while based on a boarding-house in Wilcester. For some reason known only to himself he used to play his full repertoire outside the village school at play-time. Perhaps he argued that children are notoriously generous, not realising that none of us went to school with any money in our pockets. I was not to know then that this year, 1930, was the last we would see of him and that no other organ–grinder would take his place. He and his species were about to become an extinct feature of the countryside.

Twice during the autumn a couple of caravans of gypsies passed along the lane, once coming from Avonchurch and once returning that way. A lurcher shot across the field, intent on grabbing a hare, but returned to his owner when Bouncer barked a challenge at him. I was glad that they did not choose to camp on the wide verge of the lane, as they sometimes did. They were never popular neighbours, being too light-fingered. In the old days the farmers used to be glad to employ gypsies for hoeing in summer, but now, with so much unemployment, they gave preference to local men, so there was little to keep these nomads.

Less ephemeral was the threshing outfit, which I saw slowly approaching one October afternoon. It paused to fill its tank with water from White Ox Pond – a place where, according to local legend, Mrs. Upshot had once accosted a threshing-machine driver with the admonition,

"If you must take water from thik pond, take it out of the middle. Mr. Walter Kennett's cows do drink round the outside."

The approach of the threshing-machine was like that of a cat stalking a bird or a zebra-spider approaching an unwary fly, and was about as doom-laden. It chugged ponderously along the lane, belching out black smoke and rattling its iron wheels over the flint and gravel. For the Nadderbourne farmers it was as welcome as dry weather in March or showers in May, for it meant that at last they could convert at least some of their harvest, at present stored in ricks, into cash. But I was young enough to be little concerned with the ultimate financial benefits. For me, who liked the solitary life of the open fields, with air as unpolluted as on a raft in the Atlantic, the arrival of the threshing-machine represented about four days of purgatory. With six or eight other men I would be confined to a space within ten yards of that stinking, smutty old engine, and, if the wind were in the wrong direction, enveloped in its filthy smoke. Threshing was one of the dustiest jobs imaginable, and we inevitably finished the day as black as miners at the end of an underground shift. Moreover, the dust and barley-ailes penetrated ears, nose and throats and were almost certain to trigger off a cold, even if we had avoided infection before.

To my father came the joy of thrusting his hand into the stream of golden corn emerging down a chute from the bowels of the growling machine. To me, if I could wangle it, the making of a rick of the loose straw, which kept me as far from the engine as possible. I wondered whether, in the coming year, there would be any reason for fashioning a straw cavern and whether I ought to try to make some provision for it. Nothing, however, seemed possible, without letting the other men know what I was doing; and, anyway, the future seemed as obscure as the sky through the filter of black coal-smoke.

It was a relief when the threshing-tackle, – engine, "box", elevator and hut in which the driver slept – at last pulled away from our farm and steamed away to the next. We tidied up the heaps of rubbish it left behind, and my father drove off to market, to sell his corn by sample. I suddenly remembered that, if the harvest were good, I was to have the old car for myself, but I knew better than to bank on it. The pages of *The Farmer & Stockbreeder*, which we picked up from the shop every Friday, were full of financial gloom. In that they matched my attitude to life that autumn. Of what use would a car of my own be to me, without Martita to ride by my side?

Affectionate little letters arrived from Teeta every two or three weeks. She wrote as she talked – uninhibited, effervescent, artless. I would have blushed for my mother to see them. They were full of allusions to what had happened in our halcyon summer and what she hoped would happen in the summer to come, but never a mention of any definite plans to visit England again. And college life in California was so remote from anything I knew at Nadderbourne that I felt that a hedge between us was daily growing taller and thicker. I remembered my mother's intuition, that she was not for me.

Back to ploughing in Vincent's. As the short November days slunk by, often interrupting outdoor activities with gales of rain, the work in the fields adjoining Elderberry Lane was almost ended. Well up to schedule, said my father, with satisfaction. As I ploughed the headlands in Vincent's I could see over the now bare hedgerows to Wells Piece, where Uncle Walter and Jimmy Jarman were still digging – by fits and starts. The zest seemed to have declined a little, and days sometimes passed with nary a shovelful of soil shifted. Every now and again a minor discovery provided a new, brief impetus, but the "finds" never amounted to more than an old rusty scythe-blade, some discarded cart-harness, a well-bucket with a hole in it and similar jetsam.

I took stock of the activities of Elderberry Lane as I had seen them that autumn and, guiding the plough as it carved slices of the dark earth, tried to detect in them some clue to the Secret of the Lane. What I had seen must have been typical of what Aunt Sarah would have seen, in autumn after autumn, as she surveyed the lane from her garden or cottage window. Was there anything at all which might carry a hint of treasure?

It could be nothing concerning the regular traffic of the lane – the farm workers, the two woodmen, Uncle Walter himself. The sportsmen seemed highly unlikely; they were all too preoccupied. What of the unusual characters? for me they were the Italian organ-grinder and the gypsies. Gypsies suggested possibilities; one never knew what they might be up to. But what connection they could have with sedate Aunt Sarah was more that I could fathom. Surely she was not mixed up with them? Although, of course, by all accounts, no-one knew where she came from or anything about her life before she settled in Nadderbourne. But gypsies and Aunt Sarah? – No; possible but not at all likely.

There could, of course, have been other strangers along the lane in past years. I had watched it for only two or three months; Aunt Sarah had lived there for fifty years. Uncle Walter had met the preacher there and thought he had found his treasure. When the Avonchurch cricket team came to play us at Nadderbourne, those who rode bikes generally took the short cut along Elderberry Lane. In the old days, so I had been told, charcoal-burners used to come to work in the Forest. Their ghosts were still there, so the old people said. In autumn you could see the spectral wisps of smoke rising over the trees where once their fires had burned. That was what the superstitious said, but the curls of "smoke" were only swarms of little flies engaging in courtship dances during the brief hours of sunshine.

So my mind drifted from one speculation to another, in those solitary days in the fields which were neighbouring territory to dreamland. But there was no substance in any of them. There was almost no limit to what Aunt Sarah might have seen, once during her long lifetime, but no clue as to what it might have been. Even more likely, she had seen nothing. The Secret of the Lane could well be something entirely different, and, with the year fading into darkness, we were no nearer to learning what it was.

Chapter Thirteen

The mood of sad resignation which flowed over me like a tide so frequently in the fields that autumn was not entirely unrelieved. Short days were compensated for by long evenings, and Nadderbourne had a pretty full winter programme of social activities, such as they were.

Most evenings I went down to the village hall, where I could usually find a dozen or two chaps of around my own age. It was a dusty, shabby old building, heated by an ugly, "Tortoise", slow-combustion stove. The plyboard wall panels were warped and broken, and cobwebs hung from the smoke-stained ceiling, but it was a cheerful retreat. There were facilities for playing table tennis (invariably "ping-pong" to us), darts and shove-ha'penny. The furniture included several shaky card-tables with green-baize tops, and, with luck, complete decks of cards could generally be found in one of the cupboards. Well-meaning neighbours would occasionally dump a bundle of tattered magazines, ranging from *The Field* to *The Christian Herald*, on a table, in the hope that we would find a little time for improving our minds.

Wednesday evenings we were turned out to make way for the whist players, who had a regular booking of the room throughout the winter. As that was also the evening of a "Guild" meeting at chapel, the nonconformist elders harboured a hope that those of us who didn't play whist would patronise the chapel instead, and sometimes we did, when the meeting took the form of a musical entertainment by a visiting choir or band.

On Fridays we quite frequently had a "Social", which for us meant an evening of games and entertainment (chiefly songs and dialect recitations), followed by a dance. Admission was generally a shilling a time, including refreshments, and profits, amounting to perhaps ten or twelve shillings a night, went into the coffers of the cricket club. Later in the winter, probably in early February, we would have a grand concert in aid of the cricket club, and preliminary plans were already being laid in November. But first, of course, came Christmas, with its parties and socials and, for us in Nadderbourne, its Mumming Play.

Nadderbourne was one of the few villages which preserved the medieval mumming play that, in old times, had been performed by most of the parishes in England. Someone in about the middle of the nineteenth century had taken the trouble to write down the words of our version which had otherwise been passed on by word of mouth from one generation to another from time immemorial. In consequence, after any hiatus the villagers were able to pick up the threads again and stage a revival. Such gaps frequently occurred in every village tradition. The village club, the cricket club, the village band, the mumming play, would flourish for a time and then become defunct, for some reason or another. Years later a new generation would demand a revival and would start delving in lofts, attics, outhouses and cellars to unearth old cornets, cricket nets, theatrical costumes or whatever was required. With most villages at some time or another the gap proved too wide for the mumming play ever to be resurrected, the words and drama having been forgotten. But, as I said, ours had been written down.

In 1930 the Nadderbourne Play was in full spate. We had an enthusiastic producer, Mr. William Conder, a retired schoolmaster who revelled in such things. He just took it for granted that everyone was as keen about it as he was, and so, as often happens, they were. Far from having difficulty in finding men (and a mumming play is an exclusively masculine preserve; there are no parts for women) to take the character parts, there was actually competition for them. And elements of the band insisted on providing a musical accompaniment. So rehearsals were essential, and as Christmas drew near they occupied us, in the village hall, for at least two nights a week.

We normally gave two performances of the Play, one public one in the village hall in the week before Christmas and one in Princedun

House at some time between Christmas and the New Year. This second performance was a very old tradition. I guess it dated back to a hungry age when it offered a good excuse to visit the "big house" and invite alms. Indeed, one of the characters in our play, Little Johnny Jack, had lines which made a direct appeal. Clad in tatters and hung with rag dolls he would chant,

> Here comes I Little Johnny Jack,
> With my wife and my children on my back.
> Twelve I had, but five are gone to Heaven,
> And it's soon to the Workhouse with the other seven.
> But come let us taste of your Christmas cheer,
> For Christmas comes but once a year.
> A shilling will keep us merry and bright,
> And a pot of good ale to make us sing right
> Mince pies and plum pudding are also good fare,
> Come, ladies and sirs, and now banish our care.

And then he would caper round with an old hat in his outstretched hand. By 1930 the convention had become a lump donation from the Earl – a guinea or two handed over privately at the end of the performance, as well as mince-pies and mulled cider for the whole company – but Little Johnny Jack still went through his traditional antics.

I was a little apprehensive at the prospect of making my first visit to Princedun House since having tea there with Martita back in the summer. I had no means of knowing what the keeper had told the Earl and whether I was "blacked" on that account. Nor could I know whether or not I would be recognised. It was true that the Earl and Countess had taken little notice of me, but, on the other hand, I was one of the cast and so would be in full view. I would, of course, be in costume; perhaps that would help.

Doubtless in times past our Nadderbourne Players used to tramp up the House by way of Elderberry Lane, including the lost section of it through the Forest. For the past few years, however, we had been able to rely on the bus – a racketty, primitive vehicle, equipped with wooden benches instead of seats, which we hired for such occasions. It travelled, of course, by the longer but better-surfaced road which branched off the Wilcester highway.

The Christmas expedition to Princedun House was a general outing for the people of Nadderbourne, or at least for as many as could pack into the bus. Our party included the players, the band, and umpteen supporters, including wives, sisters and girl-friends. The wives and girl-friends mostly sat on the appropriate laps; the band occupied wooden forms crammed into the corridor, thus enabling the players of strings to protect their precious instruments and the puffing-billy boys to fit in an occasional accompaniment to the singing – when we stuck to one tune long enough and with sufficient unanimity for it to be recognisable. Oh, we were a merry crowd, right enough.

Arrived at Princedun House, on a damp, misty night, we were met by the Earl and Countess, standing in the great porch and silhouetted against the golden light of the hall. Mr. Conder and a few of our leading citizens shook hands, and the rest of the crowd, including the bus driver, trooped in. I kept to the background and made my entrance with a knot of chaps, Reg Ashden with his big bassoon walking between me and the Earl.

The entrance hall of Princedun House was as big as a fair-sized Nadderbourne cottage. It provided ample space for both our players and the audience. As usual, the Earl and Countess had quite a number of house guests, as well as their immediate family. the servants had also come to watch, though a bevy of them, headed by the butler, were stationed behind a temporary bar on which were trays of mince-pies and sandwiches and a great silver bowl which, presently, would be filled with mulled cider, or cider punch or whatever it was.

A hoarse comment of, "We'd do better wi' summat to warm our gizzards avore we do start," was ignored, and we players were ushered into an ante-room to change. Mostly we were decked in costumes which, like the words, had been bequeathed from the remote past and seemed to have little to do with the characters who wore them. Most of them consisted of jerkins, trousers and hats with long coloured ribbons attached to them, so that we looked like vertically-striped zebras. King George, which was myself, wore a brass helmet (borrowed from a fireman), while the two Turkish knights had bushy black beards. The Doctor provided a contrast, in tightly buttoned black frock coat, tight, drain-pipe trousers, and a tall black hat. Father Christmas had his conventional red and white costume. All of us, except Father Christmas, had our faces blacked, which I think was part of a very old convention that the players should be so intimately identified with the characters as to be unrecognised as their workaday selves. I was King George, not Steve Maidment. And I must say I felt more at ease after the camouflage had been well applied.

Back in the hall, we found the band, or orchestra, already warming up. We had four cornets, a tenor horn, the bassoon, two fiddles, a cello, a euphonium and Uncle Walter's bass viol. Oh yes, this was not exclusively a young man's jaunt. Father Christmas was our blacksmith, Will Mould, who was sixty if he was a day and had played the part for a good twenty years past. Fred Ashden, who played the cornet in chapel on Sunday nights, was Reg's father, and Sammy Fringle, our euphonium player, was permanently bent nearly double through years spent at the cobbler's bench.

They were all seated at the end of the hall, farthest from the fire of huge logs that burned clearly on the open hearth. On either side of the fire sat the Earl and Countess and their guests. The servants and the supporters who had come with us had found chairs along the sides of the room.

Our stage was to be, as usual, a massive oak table of impressive dimensions that occupied the whole of the centre of the hall. It was both long and broad enough to allow plenty of room for action, and boxes and chairs were placed at strategic points to enable us to hop up and down smartly. The arrangement was aesthetically a satisfying one, for we performed in the middle of the audience, rather than remotely on a stage at one end of the room. It also gave scope for Father Christmas and Little Johnny Jack to caper around, bringing the spectators into the play and handing round the hat.

So we were ready to begin. The audience clapped as we trooped in, and, looking around, I thought what a perfect setting it was for a medieval drama, with the portraits of the Earl's ancestors joining the company as they gazed down from their gloomy perches on the high walls above the level of the hissing gaslight.

A word about our Mumming Play. Like all similar plays, it apparently started as a dramatic representation of the annual battle between light and darkness, between summer and winter, between life and death. Such plays therefore may well have had their origin in dim, prehistoric times, before ever the Christian religion came to Britain.

In our version, Father Christmas acted as a kind of compère, introducing each of the characters as they came on stage. Each one, as he entered, made a speech beginning, "Here comes I...." followed by a boast of what he proposed to do. After the preliminaries, the first Turkish knight leaped on to the stage and hurled challenges to all and sundry. He was the Dark Power, who now at the time of the winter solstice, was supreme.

A character identified simply as Bold Soldier took up the challenge, leaped on to the table and proceeded to fight the Turkish Knight. After a realistic duel, the Bold Soldier fell dying.

Father Christmas then called upon King George (who had evidently once been Saint George). Another duel followed, and this time it was the Turkish knight who fell wounded.

But there was a second Turkish Knight who was eager to avenge his brother. The second duel was even fiercer than the first, and King George, forced to his knees, was given a mortal blow. As he sank, dying Father Christmas shouted urgently for a doctor, which, of course, was the cue for The Doctor to enter. Like all the others, he had to make a boastful entrance speech, while his patient lay gasping, but at last he knelt down and forced some medicine between the lips of the dying champion.

Whereupon King George sprang to his feet, completely restored and ready to fight the Turkish Knight again. Father Christmas intervened, however with a speech about Christmas being a time for peace and good cheer. The band struck up an appropriate song, such as the "The British Grenadiers", and Little Johnny Jack went prancing around, performing nonsense.

From the door to the ante-room I watched the first movements of the drama. Father Christmas made his introductory speech. The first Turkish Knight, on cue, sprang on to the table and shouted his challenge.

> Here comes I, Turkish Knight,
> From heathen land I've come to fight.
> Send me now your champion bold,
> And I will make his blood run cold.

Bold Soldier accepted the challenge and fell before the Turkish Knight's wooden sword. Then it was my turn.

> Here comes I, King George, a man of courage bold;
> With this good sword I slew the dragon in days of old.
> I beat him down and drove him to the slaughter,
> And so I won the King of Egypt's daughter.
> Ah, Turkish Knight, of thee I'll mincemeat make,
> And grind thee into dust;
> And what is left of thee I'll send to the Cookshop,
> To make into mince-pie crust.

The Turkish Knight swaggered up to me and delivered his speech, ending,

> And now I'll fight King George and we shall see
> Which of us on this frosty ground will fall.

So we fought, and, after giving the clients their money's worth, the Turkish Knight collapsed on the stage, groaning,

> What hast thou done?
> That now I bleeding lie on this frosty ground?

His lament was taken up by the second Turkish Knight who, climbing on the table and standing over his colleague, exclaimed,

King George, what hast thou done?
My brother thou hast slain here on this frosty ground!
But now a man of steel am I,
And I will slash thee with my sword till thee dost die.

Whereupon he set about me in fine form, and we feinted, thrust, bashed and battered each other as realistically as we could until I deemed it time for me to collapse. Down I sank, gasping and groaning, and lay there wriggling in feigned agony, while Father Christmas shouted for a doctor.

The Doctor, who was my brother Tom, tottered in, looking this way and that to see who was calling him. He was a very good actor, was Tom, and he looked the part, with his Uncle Sam goatee beard to set off his Dickensian get-up. As he mounted the stage he launched into his introductory speech, inevitably beginning, "Here comes I....." and, inappropriately, his was one of the longest speeches in the entire play. While I supposedly lay bleeding to death he boasted at length about his "Golden Popliss drops", which would cure "palsy and quinsy, growing pains and measles, flatulence of the stomach and constipation of the bowels, gout and goitre, boils and bronchitis, warts and carbuncles", and then he demanded a fee of fifty guineas from Father Christmas before he would begin the cure.

My role was to lie there, writhing occasionally and uttering the occasional groan to let the audience know I was still alive, but not to distract attention unduly from what The Doctor and Father Christmas were saying. It was a queer, table-top-level view of the world that I had, looking up at the legs and trunks of the second Turkish Knight, The Doctor and Father Christmas towering above me, and along at the first Turkish Knight and the Bold Soldier curled in artistic heaps farther along the table.

The fire-place was behind me, and the firelight fell on the faces of the Nadderbourne supporters on the right of the table, and on the musicians at the end. I could see Sid Mould, and old Jimmy Jarman, and Helen with her brother Matt. Farther along, Les Nutbeam and John Mellish were turning their cornets over and over on their laps, wrapt in the course of the drama. The voices above my head argued and haggled. I gave another groan and kicked out with one leg. We were certainly holding the attention of our audience. Even the faces of the long-dead Earls of Crewkerne, gazing down from their dusky background, seemed alight with interest.

At the end of the line the most recent portrait, that of the late Earl, the present Earl's father, brighter and more lifelike than any of the others, having had less time than they to acquire a patina of age. From it my eye roved idly to the musicians again, to Uncle Walter, sitting patiently with his bass viol gripped between his knees.

Suddenly, in a blinding moment of revelation, I knew the Secret of the Lane. I looked again at the rather weak, kindly, vague but handsome face of the old Earl. I looked at the face of Uncle Walter. They were the same face!

Chapter Fourteen

Of the events of the rest of the evening I have little recollection. The Play must have proceeded to its ordained climax. We must have enjoyed our mince pies and mulled cider. We doubtless sang and made a hullabaloo in the bus on the way home. I cannot remember. I do recall looking at Helen and wishing I could tell her that the mystery was solved. I wished I could take her into my confidence and get her opinion as to what to do next. But she had chosen to sit on the other side of the bus, as far from me as she could get, and to try to renew our friendship was of course out of the question.

So I had to keep my own counsel and try to sort out my tumultuous thought in bed that night.

So Uncle Walter was the son of the old Earl. No wonder Aunt Sarah, speaking half to herself, had said, "If only you knew about the Secret of the Lane, what a treasure could be yours!" It could indeed. Not fools' gold in a well or a hidden cache or a patch of rare herbs, but perhaps the entire vast Princedun Estate!

Or was it, "If only you knew about the Secret Lane..." that Aunt Sarah had said. She had known, what most of the Nadderbourne villagers had forgotten, that Elderberry Lane once meant the Forest track to Princedun House, not the meandering short cut to Avonchurch. It was a path she must have known well. Did she not walk there on summer evenings, dressed in her best clothes and carrying a pretty parasol, on her way to meet her lover?

But what was I to do with my knowledge? I could not decide. I needed someone to confide in, but who? I turned over the possibilities. My father? My mother? Uncle Walter himself? Aunt Maria? The more I thought about it the more convinced I became that Aunt Maria was the proper person.

On the next Sunday afternoon, when Uncle Walter was safely at the far end of Elderberry Lane, fetching the cows, I dropped in at the cottage, nervously wondering how to tackle my self-appointed errand. Aunt Maria was sitting in her rocking–chair by a glowing grate, reading, as usual on a Sunday afternoon, *The Sunday Companion*. After a lot of prevarication, I saw nothing for it but to blurt out the truth,

"Aunt Maria, when we were up at the House with the Mumming Play last week I looked at Uncle Walter, sitting near the portrait of the old Earl, and their faces were the same!"

She heard me out, as I went into details. Then for a time she sat with her hands folded over the paper on her aproned lap, looking at me with steady eyes.

It's true," I assured her, faltering a little before her gaze.

"I know'" she said.

"You – you *know*?"

"Yes," she said, sighing. "I've known for a long , long, time."

"Does Uncle Walter?"

"Oh no, indeed he doesn't. And don't you on any account tell him, whatever you do."

"I can see, Steve," she went on, rising and going to a cupboard, "that, seeing you know so much, you had better know it all. But promise me that you will never, ever, breathe a word to anyone about this and about what I am going to show you now."

From the depths of the cupboard she extracted a big family Bible, so heavy she had difficulty in lifting it. It had gilt-edged pages and its black leather covers, deeply embossed with gold, were fastened with a gilt clip. She laid it on the table and, opening it, revealed on the inside of the front cover a kind of secret pocket, intended apparently for holding papers. From it she took several envelopes, one made of a kind of parchment, with a cross of pink tape.

"Aunt Sarah, my mother-in-law, gave me all this soon after our silver wedding anniversary. When she did she said,

"I ought to burn it all, Maria, but I haven"t the heart to. I must share my secret with someone, and I've known you long enough to know that you will never tell Walter, for his sake."

And then she told me what I am going to tell you."

I promised that never a word about it would pass my lips.

"Well, not until everyone concerned is long dead," Aunt Maria amended. "After that, I must leave it to your judgment."

"Aunt Sarah came from a village in Devonshire. Her father was a small farmer. Her mother died when Sarah was about twelve. There was an older sister who stayed at home to look after the house, so when Sarah left school she was put out to service. She moved from one place to another and eventually fell in with a very good family, who made her governess to their two small children. In the meantime, her father died, so she never afterwards went back to Devon.

The family took her to India, where one of the children died and the other sickened. I suppose it was the climate. Anyway, they decided to send this second little girl back to her grandparents in England. The father was in the Army, and the mother chose to stay with him, so Sarah had the responsibility of bringing the child home.

The ship sprung a leak somewhere in the Indian Ocean and only just managed to limp into Cape Town harbour. There Sarah had to stay with the little girl for several weeks, waiting for another boat. Fortunately she had addresses of friends of the family in the town and so was well looked after. During those weeks she met the Earl of Crewkerne, who was then a young man – and quite handsome, I may tell you.

His lordship came home on the same ship as Sarah, and the pair of them fell in love.

Lord Crewkerne was impetuous, and like all these aristocrats he liked to have his own way – at once. He wanted to get married there and then.

"The ship's captain will do it." he told Sarah. Somehow he prevailed on the man to perform a ceremony. Whether it was valid or not, I don't know, but certainly it was performed. Here's the certificate he gave the Earl."

She took it from an envelope and passed it to me. It was a handwritten document, certifying, in ink faded brown with age, that Henry Algernon Vavasour Sinclair-Penhammett, bachelor, had been lawfully married to Sarah Kennett, spinster, on S.S. *Tahiti Princess* on July 11th, 1865.

The Earl had married under his family name, not having then succeeded to the title.

"At that time it didn't appear that he ever would become Earl," Aunt Maria explained. "He had an elder brother, who died a year or so later."

"He was not a very brave man," Aunt Maria went on, "and he had a mother who was a right tartar. He was really scared of her.

Well, when they landed in England and Sarah had safely delivered the little girl to her grandparents, he installed her in a flat in London, where in due course your Uncle Walter was born. The Earl, as I feel I must call him though he was still just the Honourable Henry Penhammett, kept telling her he would tell his mother as soon as the time was right, but then, it never was right. And what happened next made it almost impossible.

Henry's elder brother died, and Henry became heir to the Estate. And then he very soon found out that there wouldn't be an estate to be heir to for much longer, if he didn't do what was required of him. The place had run downhill so badly, for some reason or another, that it was absolutely necessary for him to marry an heiress. That is what his elder brother was going to do, and that is what he now had to do. The old Lady Crewkerne had got so far as to look out a bride for him. Lady Emma Battesley, the daughter of the Earl of Yarlington. There was plenty of money in that family, and Lady Emma was an heiress in her own right.

That put Henry in a proper quandary. If he hadn't been man enough to face up to his mother then, he certainly couldn't now. Fancy! having to tell that old dragon that he had married the penniless daughter of a smallholder! and with all the family estates at stake! I don't know what went on between him and Sarah, but, whether he got her agreement or not, he married Lady Emma in a big society wedding in London. And about the same time Aunt Sarah brought little Walter down here, to live in the cottage along the lane. It was Princedun property then, of course, so that was easy to arrange. He had it made over to her. The deeds are in there.

"But that made the Earl a bigamist," I pointed out.

"Right enough," agreed my aunt. "But whether legally so I don't know. There seems to be a bit of doubt about these marriages at sea back in the last century. The certificate looks all right; it's properly signed and witnessed; but it's handwritten, not on a printed form. I couldn't say. I think your Aunt Sarah was doubtful about it, too."

"So she was content to live in the cottage and let another woman be Countess of Crewkerne,"

"Yes. Your Aunt Sarah was a remarkable woman. Besides, I think she truly loved him."

She must have done. But, granted that, I could appreciate that, once the wedding had taken place, she had little to gain by making awkward revelations. Branding the Earl as a bigamist would have ruined the family, broken up the estate, probably sent him to prison and also most likely have killed his love for her. Anything saved from the wreck would have gone to the lawyers. And so she accepted her role and tried to be content with clandestine meetings in the woods, along the old Elderberry Lane.

How long it would have lasted cannot be known, for soon came the tragedy of the death of the Earl. That shot? Was it really an accident? Or suicide? or murder?

"Murder, I think," said Aunt Maria, quite calmly.

"At least , we always thought so."

"You see," she explained, "when Lady Emma married and came to live at Princedun she brought the Upshots with her. There happened to be a vacancy for a head-keeper just then, and it seemed a sensible thing to do. The Upshots had been in the service of the Battesleys for hundreds of years – more or less worshipped the family like gods. You know how it is sometimes, with these old families.

So, supposing old Adam Upshot, in Princedun woods at night, happens to see what goes on between the Earl and Sarah. Suppose he does this more than once. Suppose he creeps near enough to hear them talking and realises or suspects what the real relationship between them is. He was the sort of man who, out of loyalty to Lady Emma, would be quite prepared to shoot the unfaithful husband and make it appear as an accident."

I remembered what my mother had told me about Mrs. Upshot.

"Do you think Mrs. Upshot knew?" I asked.

"I think she guessed. But she was too scared of those two menfolk of hers to do more than hint about it. But I think it was on her mind."

"So that was why old Adam Upshot was so bitter about Aunt Sarah."

"Of course. He must have hated her. And, besides, he must have known that she suspected him. He could never be entirely at ease while she lived."

"And what about Uncle Walter through all this? Didn't he ever know anything?"

"Never a thing. Aunt Sarah was tempted when the Earl was killed. She thought that perhaps it was her duty to tell all she knew. Then she thought of all the trouble it would cause, and so she kept quiet. As Walter grew up, she sometimes wondered whether she ought to act for his sake. But when she looked at him she knew better. You've seen the portrait of the old Earl, and you've heard me say he was a weak character. Your Uncle Walter is just like him, in character as well as looks! Can't you imagine him as Earl of Crewkerne! If ever a man would be out of his depth, he would have been.

Your Aunt Sarah did what she thought best for her son."

I thought of Uncle Walter, taking his cows for their leisurely stroll down Elderberry Lane and back, every day for all those years. Of Uncle Walter, leaning on a gate and smoking his old pipe, at peace with the world. Of Uncle Walter making music on his bass viol, a unit in the band and in the rustic society of Nadderbourne. Of Uncle Walter searching for his treasure and of his joy at finding it within himself. I thought of Aunt Sarah, looking out of her cottage day by day and watching him pass. Of her pleasure at seeing him marry a country girl, Aunt Maria, and settle down next door.

The thoughts kept me silent for several minutes, and presently Aunt Maria, watching me and sensing what was going through my mind, put in,

"Yes, Steve; it's a good life here in Nadderbourne, you know. None better. Your Aunt Sarah was content. And your Uncle Walter, though he doesn't know it, has been happier than ever he would have been as Earl of Crewkerne."

"Yes, can't you imagine it?" she said, with a broad smile. "Me, a countess."

She became serious.

"There have been times," she admitted, a trifle wistfully, "when I thought it would have been nice."

"But," she added firmly, "I did what was best for your Uncle Walter."

Lucky Uncle Walter! To have not one but two women in his life who were willing to keep a secret like that to preserve his happiness. Young as I was I was impressed. It is only in later years that I have come to appreciate how wise and truly remarkable they were.

"After our twenty-fifth wedding anniversary," said Aunt Maria, "your Aunt Sarah had the property and most of her money made over to me, so that very little would appear in her will when she died. She didn't want anyone, and especially not your Uncle, to know that she was quite well off."

I caught sight of a bank book in the pocket of the Bible, with the other papers, but did not see inside it then. Its contents were only revealed years later, when both Uncle Walter and Aunt Maria died and their estate came into our family. Aunt Maria left not only the deeds of the two cottages, the meadows and orchard but also a bank balance of £6,500, – a very substantial sum in those days. The old Earl had been as generous to Aunt Sarah as he had dared.

The short afternoon had passed. Aunt Maria had to light the oil lamp to see how to put the big Bible away in its cupboard.

"Your Uncle Walter will soon be back," she said. "I've told you all this, partly because you had discovered so much and needed to know the rest, and partly because it will be yours one day, I suppose. I mean, you're the eldest Maidment son, so one day the papers and the property and all the rest will come to you. Take care of it. And not a word about it mind."

I promised.

Out into the chilly air, with a hint of sleet on the northwest wind, I decided to walk down Elderberry Lane and home across the meadows rather than take the direct route up the hill to our farm. By Noah's Close I met Uncle Walter sauntering along with the cows, so we had concluded our talk without too much time to spare.

"Evening, Uncle. Snow about ?" I greeted him.

"Shouldn't wonder," grunted the rightful Earl of Crewkerne. "It's cold enough to freeze a brass monkey."

So he would trudge back now to his little farmstead and crouch down under the flanks of each cow, one after another, his head tucked against her warm abdomen as he milked, by the yellow light of an oil lantern. Then he would plod indoors, take off his heavy boots, and sit down to a meal of bread and butter and Aunt Maria's home-made lardy cake, before changing to go to chapel with his bass viol. And Aunt Maria would clear away the tea-things, wash up in an old enamel bowl, put the table cloth with the rest of the week's washing outside the back door in readiness for another cold morning at the wash-tub tomorrow, and then she too would go upstairs and put on her bonnet, preparing to accompany Uncle Walter to the service.

Yet she had only to open her mouth and tell all she knew, and she could perhaps exchange this routine for that of the chatelaine of Princedun House, with a butler and a battalion of maids to obey every signal of her little finger. Or, if her revelations caused a major catastrophe in the Crewkerne fortunes, there would be at least enough left for she and Uncle to live a life of comparative luxury.

Both she and Aunt Sarah had thought their choice was the right one. But both had known that Uncle Walter would not agree, and so they kept from him the Secret of the Lane. I know now that they were wise. Then I was not so sure.

As I walked in the late December dimpsey past Noah's Close and Austin's, past the ruined cottage that had been Aunt Sarah's home, past Stony Lawn, and Vincent's, and White Ox Pond (now with a film of ice around its margins), and the keeper's cottage, and into the shade of the leafless oaks and hazels of Hobbit's Copse, I thought a little ruefully of our abortive attempts to solve the problem of the Secret Lane. Of how we had followed what appeared to be a lead in investigating the herbs and plants that grew by the lane; of how excited we had been at the finding of treasure in Golden Cap Tump; of the discovery of fools' gold in Aunt Sarah's disused well; of our probing with the help of the Professor into the clues offered by the names of the fields and woods of Nadderbourne; of how we listened to the testimony of Uncle Walter concerning the inner peace he had found.

And then I realised, with a flash of intuition, that we had come nearest to the Secret of the Lane when we had not been searching for it at all. It was when Teeta and I had clung together, naked in the bracken, in the warm summer twilight. For doing so we had duplicated what must have happened between the old Earl (then the young Earl!) and Sarah those many years before (even, it seems, to having been spied upon by Keeper Upshot!) The best secrets of life can only be discovered by living.

I thought again of Aunt Sarah, that serene, solitary lady, living for fifty-three years in her little cottage by Elderberry Lane. Of the apparent narrow limits of her restricted routine. Of the secret she had kept for all those years. Of her brutal death.

Was it a tragedy? Was it all waste? What had her life been worth, after all?

Then, as I paused to gaze over the gate (padlocked again!) that barred the way into the Elderberry Lane through the Forest, I caught in the eye of memory the vision of Teeta dancing to meet me through the nightjar-haunted glade. I felt the curves of her body, wrapped her rippling black hair around my naked shoulders, kissed and kissed her again and again, while around us the ghost moths fluttered noiselessly, and the nightjars clattered, and the soft-winged owl hooted as it drifted away into woods heavy with the sweet scent of honeysuckle. Teeta had gone now, but I wouldn't have missed that experience for the whole world.

And I knew that for Aunt Sarah, too, it had all been worth while. For she, too, had known what it was to walk, with airy, eager step, to meet her lover in the luminous twilight of the summer woods by Elderberry Lane.

Epilogue

The spiralling seasons brought spring again to Nadderbourne, but Martita remained as far away as ever. Her letters, addressed to "My sweet, my darling Steve", were still loving and naughty, but they arrived less frequently. And when she had finished with recapitulating memories, she wrote of people and places and experiences of which I knew nothing. It seemed most unlikely that she would be allowed to visit Princedun again this year.

I am a faithless and impatient lover. I cannot live on memories, however pleasant. I need a warm human presence to share experiences with me – someone to admire, to kiss, to tease, to link arms with me, to nag me.

I was beginning to make the grade with Helen again. After an interlude of going around with Harold Nutbeam during the winter she had thrown him over (and that wasn't to be wondered at – the big, fat slob!), and so, with both of us at a loose end, we had drifted together. We had reached the stage of walking decorously arm-in-arm again down Elderberry Lane on Sunday afternoons. I hadn't yet attempted to put my arm around her waist and kiss her, but I intended to soon.

So on a sunny May afternoon I sat under the big maple in Austin's and scribbled a poem of renunciation:–

> The sun warms brake and meadow, –
> As I sit once again
> Beneath the maple's shadow
> By Elderberry Lane.

I will breathe in the fragrance
Of the lilac and the may,
And the bees that pass as vagrants
Shall bear my thoughts away

To another magic summer;
And I shut my eyes to see
The raven–haired newcomer
Who shared its joys with me.

Yet though I play with fancy,
And though my heart be fain,
The vision that enchants me –
It will not come again.

It's another road I'm taking
From which I shall not rove,
Although I know the aching
Of a divided love.

Life is not dreams but doing –
But today I dream until
The sun, the clouds pursuing,
Is lost behind the hill.

That is what I wrote, and it made me feel quite noble and heroic. Tired with the effort of composition and melancholy through expressing those self–sacrificial sentiments, I got up, stretched myself and trudged back across Austin's to the farm. But as I went a small, insistent inner voice told me,

"Steve, you're a fraud! If Martita were to appear around the corner now you'd be into her arms in an instant, and be damned to Helen!"

And I knew it was true. I'm sorry, Helen!